Melanie Tem's first published works were short fiction in various literary and small magazines and non-fiction articles in professional journals. Her stories have more recently appeared in *Isaac Asimov's Science Fiction Magazine* and in the anthologies *Women of Darkness, Women of the West,* and *Skin of the Soul* (The Women's Press, 1990); stories will soon appear in the magazines *Fantasy Tales, Whispers* and *Cemetery Dance* and in the anthologies *Final Shadows, Cold Shocks,* and *Copper Star.* Her first novel *Prodigal,* is published in Dell Publishing's new Abyss line. *Blood Moon* is her second novel.

A social worker with background in nursing homes, child abuse, and disabilities, Melanie Tem lives in Denver, Colorado, with her husband, the writer Steve Rasnic Tem, and their four chidren.

BLOOD MOON

MELANIE TEM

THE
WOMEN'S
PRESS

First published in Great Britain by The Women's Press Limited
A member of the Namara Group
34 Great Sutton Street,
London EC1V 0DX.

British Library Cataloguing-in-Publication Data: A catalogue record
for this book is available from the British Library.

ISBN 0 7043 4272 3

Typeset by
Ponting-Green Publishing Services,
Sunninghill, Berkshire.

Printed and bound in Great Britain by
BPCC Hazell Books
Aylesbury, Bucks
Member of BPCC Ltd

For Christopher,
who knows.

And, of course,
for Steve

Acknowledgements

My thanks to:

Peter Vargas, MD, Shirley Dickinson, RN, and Susan Zimmerman, MSW, for their technical assistance.

The members of the Northern Colorado Writers' Workshop and of Milford Minor 1982, for their critical support.

Steve, my live-in-editor and the love of my life, without whom, I think, no words would ever be the right ones.

1

Breanne Novak picked up the photos again and ran her fingertips across them, as though she might feel something she could not see. He was a stocky, dark-haired boy with a round face and a smile she could only think to describe as self-possessed. At the same time there was something terrible about his eyes, which did not quite meet the camera.

With a start she recognised it – she had lived with it all her life. Anger. Enormous anger. She thought she'd escaped it by finally growing up, but here was this child. Summoning her. Daring her to try again. She looked into his eyes through the gloss of the photo and wondered if she'd ever be able to see any further than that.

Gregory. Her son's name was Greg.

Breanne glanced across the table at the social worker and guessed that there would be no clinical justification for the clear, bright affirmation she had already made: that this was a child meant to be her own.

'He's an interesting child,' Melinda was saying. 'He's got a lot of things going for him. Intelligence. Charm. Survival instincts.'

'But,' said Breanne, and waited. After several months of working with the long-haired, sweet-faced, iron-willed Melinda on the home study that had finally qualified her as a prospective adoptive parent, she felt free to be a little bold. Just a little, though, for Breanne was very aware of how much power the social worker had over her life.

'But,' Melinda agreed, almost reluctantly. 'There is something about him. It's hard to pin down. Almost mysterious.'

'I guess eleven-year-olds can be pretty mysterious,' Breanne said, glancing again at the photo under her hand.

Melinda nodded seriously. 'Things – *happen* when Greg is around. His birthmother relinquished him and kept the little girl. All kinds of things get broken, yet you can't really say he's destructive because you never *see* him break anything. Other kids are getting hurt or getting into trouble all the time when he's in the home, yet you can't put your finger on just what it is he does. He's been asked to leave every foster home he's ever been in and there have been a lot of them. More than once, the foster parents have called me and demanded that I get him that day.'

'Why?' Breanne was indignant.

'Because things just don't go right when Greg is there. He's got so much anger. He seems to be almost totally unattached.'

'Of course he's "got anger." He's lost his mother and a series of stepfathers and his little sister. Of course he's "unattached." I'd be unattached, too. What do people expect?'

'People expect,' Melinda said evenly, eyeing her, 'that their kids will give them something in return. Gratitude. Respect. Loyalty. At least love.'

'That's a mistake,' Breanne said flatly, and found herself staring with renewed interest at the picture of the self-possessed, utterly forlorn little boy.

'The foster mom says he never asks about his sister, Sherry. He doesn't seem to mind at all that they were split up.' Melinda paused. 'Greg doesn't seem to give a damn about anybody. It's as if he spends all his energy being furious with the world and doesn't have any left over for getting close. Anger is the only consistent thing he's ever had, and he'll hold onto it with a vengeance. Don't go into this lightly, Breanne. He won't be an easy kid.'

Breanne nodded and lowered her eyes. She liked Melinda, even felt a tentative alliance with her, but the nature of the social worker's job required a certain arrogance which Breanne found offensive.

'Because of his experiences with abusive men,' Melinda went on more gently, 'we thought he'd do well with a single mom.'

Breanne smiled. None of that mattered. The little face in the photograph was demanding her attention. She felt her throat painfully constrict, her breath grow ragged, as if small hands were tearing at her already. The narrowed eyes seemed to follow her. Her son, waiting.

Greg rode the bicycle furiously around the farmyard again, veering to chase chickens and cats, swerving dangerously to jump over the biggest stones he could find. It wasn't his bike, of course, but they'd said he could use it while he lived here and it wasn't broken yet.

The social worker's car was in the driveway. The social worker was in the house, talking to Mrs Decker. He didn't like social workers. They took things away from you. They said one thing and did something else. They took Sherry away from him because he was bad.

The bike skidded in the hot, dry gravel and he almost fell. He caught himself at the last minute, dragging his sneaker so hard that some of the rubber peeled off. He wished he hadn't caught himself. He wished he'd fallen hard, wrecked the bike and smashed his face up good.

They were going to make him leave this place. He knew the signs. It was because Mrs Decker didn't like him anymore. The social worker talked about 'adoption' and 'a forever mom,' and she had tried to get him to look at pictures in an album, but he knew better than to believe anything a social worker said. It wouldn't be any different this time. He could be bad enough to make anybody send him away.

Randy came out of the barn with the milk pail in his hand. Randy was the oldest of the Decker foster kids, but he was retarded, and so a lot of the time he acted like a two-year-old in a six-foot-tall body. All at once Greg hated him. He swung the bike into the other boy's path, stopped three feet in front of him, and glared. The handle of the pail broke and milk spilled full on the ground, soaking Randy's feet and pantlegs. Randy yelped. Greg whooped in triumph and took off on the bike again, down the dirt lane that circled behind the barn.

He wasn't going in there again. The woman he'd seen with the social worker was the one who thought she was going to 'adopt' him. Thought she was going to be his damn mother. He had one mother. He remembered her. She sent him away because he was bad.

He flung himself into the scratchy weeds behind the barn and let the blue bike fall over onto its side. He listened for them to call him, but nobody did. He waited for somebody to come around the barn looking for him and he plotted his escape, down the lane to the pasture and the pond, but nobody came. He was not going in there. He waited a boy's eternity – fifteen, twenty minutes, half an hour.

Slowly he got to his feet. The anger inside him was hotter than the July afternoon, and he was sweating. But now the anger didn't quite fill him. There was also a thin, warm feeling that he didn't want to have. Curiosity. Need. He scowled. He started to walk toward the house. Then he stopped. He looked over his shoulder at the bike lying in the skunkweed, stared at it, and heard with satisfaction the small hiss as each of its tires went flat, the pop as the chain broke.

She looked just like her picture. The social worker had left the album on his bed, even though he'd told her not to, and he'd let himself flip through it once before it got torn apart. She had brown hair and brown eyes lighter than his own. Her hands moved when she talked, a fact which surprised him because it hadn't been in the pictures. She was tall. He liked that. When he realised that he liked that, he was immediately infuriated. He wondered if she hit, or grounded, or made you kneel in a corner like Mrs Decker. He wondered if she could make spaghetti. He wondered what 'adoption' was. He was not going in there.

He had been standing behind the kitchen door peering through the crack, and two plates on the counter behind him had just shattered, when Randy came in and yelled, 'Here he is!' Then they came and got him. He wouldn't look at her. But she smiled and talked to him quietly and everybody else left the room. She gave him a crystal, a little heavy piece of glass that broke the sunlight up into rainbows. Fascinated, he held it up to his eye and watched the sunlight break and break again as he turned his head. He tried to think about the crystal breaking in his hand, drawing his blood for her to see, but he couldn't. He was suddenly too tired, too scared, too lonely, and the crystal was too solid.

She came beside him to look at the rainbows with him, and she put her arm around him, and Greg, despite himself, looked up at her and leaned his head just slightly against her shoulder and smiled.

2

Andy Novak sat upright in his chair. In his hand a cup of herbal tea; he didn't like the taste of it, but he had read somewhere that it wouldn't disturb his sleep. Behind his neck was the hard, cylindrical pillow Ruth had made for him just before she died, one of a series over the years that helped to control his headaches. But now it wasn't working. In the months since Ruth had died the headaches had been worse than he could ever remember, and he'd had them all his life. Now nothing he did seemed to dilute them.

Which was as it should be, he caught himself thinking. He moved his head a fraction of an inch, and the room twisted and spun and plummeted like an airplane out of control. His vision contorted. His stomach wrenched. His head raged, the pain so total and so familiar after seventy-odd years that it was like something inside him with a life of its own, clamoring to get out.

He knew what would happen if it did. All his life he had known, since he was five years old and his parents and his brother John had died one after the other in the 1917 flu epidemic and he'd had to go live with his Uncle Clarence on the farm and his little sister Mary had gone somewhere else to live and he'd never seen her again. They'd told him, 'Don't cry.'

So he didn't. Something terrible would happen if the hurt got out, so he'd kept it inside his own head, fighting it, the headaches threatening to break him even then. From that time on he'd tried to imagine what would happen to the world if his pain ever got out, if they ever knew the things he knew. The older he got the more he imagined it, in vivid and accumulating detail, and so the headaches got worse.

Andy gripped the wooden arms of his chair as he had a hundred times before, his fingers fitting into the polished grooves. He would not lie down. He would not cry out. He would not give in. The older he got the worse it was, the more he saw that the world at large was in a mess from which it would never recover, and the more fragile and essential seemed his protection, his power, his control.

Wars everywhere. Economic disaster. Rape and murder. Andy gripped the arms of his chair and forced his eyes to stay open against the pain. Teenage pregnancy. Drug abuse. And now she was adopting that boy.

'Daddy.' She'd looked at him as if she was afraid of him. That look had always irritated him. He'd never hurt her in her life. He'd always kept himself from hurting her, and her fear of him was a betrayal. He tightened his lips and looked away. 'Daddy, I've got something exciting to tell you.'

She was adopting that boy. By herself. He didn't understand why she would do that without a man. He didn't understand why she'd never married, although he was relieved by that. His younger daughter Claire lived so far away and had been married so many times that he had deliberately lost track. He hardly thought of her at all anymore, especially since Ruth wasn't around to bring up her name, although both girls were equally provided for in his will.

That child. A child with all those problems. A child not her own.

'I hope you've thought this through,' he said to her, not trusting himself to say any more. He glanced at the picture she held out to him, intending to look at it only long enough to show her the enormity of his disapproval. His love for her was so much like anger that he dared not let it loose or it would destroy them both.

7

But when he glanced at the face of the boy in the picture, something made him stare. This boy was dangerous. This boy would hurt her.

'That's Greg,' said Breanne, her voice a little unsteady. 'That's your new grandson.'

'He's not mine,' Andy said, pushing the picture away and seeing with horror the pain on his daughter's face. So like her mother's, so unlike his own. They didn't know what real pain was. 'You do what you want. That boy will never be mine.'

But he was. Andy had known it the moment he saw the picture, and he knew it now as he sat waiting in his chair with the headache pulsing inside him and the television show going on. She was bringing the boy here today to meet him. She had insisted. He wouldn't know what to say. But he had recognised something in that round face, those huge brown eyes, that self-possessed smile, and he could take on no more.

' . . .double-digit inflation,' said the man on the screen. 'Prime rate climbing again . . .home ownership down . . .'

Andy listened. He put together his own, much worse, interpretation of the economic situation, and felt the pain slip its hold a little.

They were knocking on his door. For a moment Andy could not move. To move would be to invite something dangerous in, to open a crack through which something dangerous could seep out, or at the very least to make his headache worse. Andy scowled. He pulled himself out of his chair. His headache pounded, but he had to admit it had abated somewhat, gone back into hiding. He straightened his shoulders, lifted his chin. He smoothed the bright-red turtleneck and the red plaid pants over his slight frame. He practiced a smile.

'Daddy!' Breanne exclaimed when he answered the door. 'I was starting to worry.'

He smiled at her, keeping his hands at his sides. War, he thought furiously. Rape, and in a flashing image saw it happening to her, saw himself tracking down and castrating her assailants. Car accidents, teenage drunk drivers hurtling down the wrong side of the road. He had been chronically annoyed with Ruth because she, in her simple way, didn't worry so much. No matter what was going on in their daughters' lives, or what they imagined was going on, Ruth had always been able to sleep.

Andy didn't dare look at his daughter when he was loving her like this. He didn't dare, of course, look at the husky little boy standing beside her. So he focused his gaze on a point just over her head and said quietly, 'I was watching a program about the economy. I tell you, I don't know how we're going to get out of this. It's worse than the Depression, much worse. Of course, it doesn't affect me. I'm not worried personally. I've got a good pension and not many years left to live. But it will affect you.' Saying all that, he felt the pain loose its grip a little more, saw the savage reds and browns of it pale a little inside his head.

'Daddy,' said Breanne, ignoring his important statements as she so often did now that she was grown up, though when she was little she'd loved to discuss things with him and he'd reveled in the pliability and spark of her mind. 'Daddy, I'd like you to meet my son. Greg.'

The boy hung back. With an effort Andy lowered his eyes to the sullen, frightened little face, and, after a moment, stiffly held out his hand. 'Pleased to meet you, Greg,' he said, and the boy's name would scarcely pass his lips.

The boy would not shake hands. He would not even look up. He turned away from them both and scuffed hard with the toe of his shoe at Andy's newly painted porch. Outraged, his headache back full force, Andy considered dropping his hand and retreating into the dark, lonely house, leaving them to follow him or go away or do whatever they would, when Breanne said firmly, 'Greg. Stop kicking and shake hands with your grandfather.'

At once the boy stopped kicking. He raised his head and shot Breanne a look of such directed malevolence that Andy wanted to pull away from it, to take himself well out of its reach. He did not. He knew better than to give in to

9

that anger, that fear, in any of its forms, even when it belonged to someone else.

The boy took the one step required for him to just reach Andy's hand and clasped it, hard. He raised his dark, furious, powerful eyes to Andy's face, and Andy caught his breath.

3

Wet dark alone he cried nobody came he cried he cried and then somebody came a voice a shadow he didn't know he cried he kicked his legs a thing a big thing a thing as big as his head came out of the darkness and then the side of his head hurt hurt he cried the thing came again he turned his head and this time it was his ear the back of his head places he wasn't sure even belonged to him hurt hurt he cried he cried and then he stopped crying because he couldn't breathe.

'Stop your crying, you little bastard!' A voice he didn't know not his mother not her he held his breath.

'A man can't get a decent night's sleep around here with that screaming kid.'

'He's just a baby, Jimmy. Honey, he's only six months old.' His mother's voice Greg let out his breath and opened his mouth to cry again but he didn't.

'Listen. If I'm gonna stay here he's gonna have to learn fast. He ain't even mine, for Chrissake. I don't have to put up with this shit.'

'I know, Jimmy. I know you don't.'

They left him then the bad voice the hurting thing his mother's voice everything left him wet dark alone Greg let out a tiny wail a hiccup and then fell asleep.

'Goddammit, I'm gonna bust your butt!'

The man grabbed him and turned him over his knee. Greg was already screaming; the man had hurt his arm.

The man pulled down his wet pants. The belt sang and his bottom hurt so bad he wet himself all over again and got the man's lap wet and the man swore at him threw the belt turned him over threw him onto the floor. Greg was shrieking.

'Les, honey, don't. He's just a little boy. You'll wake the baby.'

'He's three years old. Old enough to know not to piss his pants. If he won't stop it I will.'

'What are you going to do?' His mother's voice, frightened, all the way across the room.

Greg's pants were still down around his knees. The man loomed over him. The man grabbed Greg's penis and pulled it out straight. Greg yelled but tried not to move, tried to hold himself very still.

'You better not fight me, sonny boy, or I'll pull it out by the roots.'

He will he will Mama. Greg's screaming had become a high-pitched wail and inside his terror his revulsion at having been a bad boy *again* was something new, something that showed him for the first time in his life that he was separate from this man and from all the men with the strange voices and the hard hands and even from his mother. An anger.

His penis hurt. Something was wrapped around it.

'There,' said the man. 'That oughta stop it.'

'Les, for God's sake – '

Still waiting, Greg managed to raise his head a little and look down at himself. His penis was pink, upright, and something he couldn't see was wrapped tight around it. Hurt, hurt, a horror at what was happening to him, a growing sickness in his stomach, an anger. Panic-stricken, he felt rather than saw a thin stream of pale-yellow pee trickle out of the end of his penis as if it didn't belong to him.

'You want it tighter, huh? That what you want?' The man twisted the rubber band again and let it snap back against Greg's tiny balls.

Greg shrieked and suddenly the new thing, the anger,

was everything and he was shrieking right at the man whose big hand had struck the floor between his legs. In his mind he saw blood, saw broken things, and the man yelled and jerked his hand away and Greg saw a thin, bright line of blood across the man's knuckles.

'Greg.'

The whisper at his door was familiar. Greg turned over in bed. He had stayed up late reading Superman comic books with a flashlight under his covers, and he had just fallen asleep when the whisper found him.

'Greg, it's me. Uncle Roy.'

'Yeah. I know who it is.'

'Well, aren't you glad to see me?'

'No.'

But in fact he sort of was. This man was nicer to him than any of the others had been. In the daytime Uncle Roy never yelled at him, never hit him, hardly seemed to notice him at all, and the nighttime visits weren't all that bad.

Uncle Roy crossed the room quietly and sat down on Greg's bed. Greg could tell from the sound of her breathing that Sherry was awake in the other bed. Uncle Roy put his hand inside the front of Greg's pajamas, as he had done many times before, and Greg, knowing that nothing was expected of him, lay back against the pillow and almost fell asleep again. Uncle Roy was breathing hard. He always did.

But all at once something was different. Uncle Roy was sitting up on Greg's bed, doing something with his pants. He pulled them off over his shoes and dropped them onto the floor, and Greg saw in astonishment the huge swelling thing rising out of the man's pubic hair, like nothing he had, like nothing he had ever seen or imagined. He felt a hand on the back of his neck, felt himself being twisted and turned over Uncle Roy's lap, and thought he was going to be spanked. For what? For reading comics after bedtime, maybe. For teaching Sherry things. The anger and fear filled him like blood, turned the insides of his eyelids flame red, made his heart race and his breath come hard.

13

'Ah,' said Uncle Roy softly. 'You like it, too, don't you? I thought you would.'

Greg had opened his mouth as wide as he could to breathe around the anger, and now there was something in it. Uncle Roy's thing, hard and tasting like salt and big so big it was making him gag. He tried to turn his head away but Uncle Roy held him there the hand on the back of his neck hurting hurting the thing in his mouth making him sick the red hot anger filling him till he knew he would burst.

Suddenly Uncle Roy arched his back and threw his hands back against the headboard and gasped, and slimy stuff came into Greg's mouth and he was sure he was going to throw up. Dimly he wished he would, puke all over Uncle Roy's big hairy thing. But he had heard – with awful, satisfying clarity – something snap. The noise echoed in his head and some of his anger seemed to spurt away as Uncle Roy cried out. The hand left Greg's neck and he rolled off the bed onto the floor.

'My hand! Jesus Christ, my hand's broken!' As he opened the door Greg saw that he was holding one hand funny, away from his body and up in the air, as if it hurt.

Seeing that, Greg felt things he did not understand. Bad things, hateful things, but things that felt good. The door closed. He lay on the floor – dirty, betrayed, excited. From the sound of her breathing he knew that Sherry was awake, and excited, too.

4

Greg perched on the tall metal stool in the corner of the kitchen. Breanne hated having people around while she cooked, but she gritted her teeth and answered most of his questions with minimal irritation: 'What *is* that stuff? Don't you think you should put a lid on that pot? Can I stir that?'

She was glad she'd let him stay in the kitchen, for this seemed to have become their first tradition. A family tradition. With the wistful self-consciousness of any new parent, Breanne wondered whether he would remember this when he was grown up and gone. 'I used to sit on a tall metal stool in the kitchen while my mother cooked, and we used to talk.'

They did talk. About pro football, punk rock, video games. They had never once talked about his birthmother or his little sister, Sherry. They had not talked about his problems in school, his lack of friends, his temper. They hadn't talked about sex, either – although, to her own amusement, she was ready for that one. They talked about the reruns of *Gilligan's Island* and *I Love Lucy* that he liked to watch after school, and sometimes Breanne struggled not simply to tune him out when she wanted to study a recipe or, tonight, worry about the fact that her father was coming to dinner.

In their few months together Breanne had learned not to ask her son direct questions, even about innocent subjects. Confronted with anything – his predictions for the Broncos' season, say – his whole body would stiffen and seem to compact, and into his eyes would come flooding the look she already knew so well and couldn't quite name – hunted, frightened, enraged.

Dangerous.

So she was careful. She was determined – for his sake, and her father's, and her own – to do it right this time. She said things to invite rather than to draw him out. She said things – so far, little things – about herself. She engaged in what the social worker called 'guerrilla warfare' – dropping brief, rehearsed statements and then letting him do with them what he would.

'Your homework is between you and the teacher. But if you fail, they'll make you go to summer school.'

'You've been through a lot of changes in the past few months. Maybe you just don't have any energy left for making friends.'

'Anger can be useful if you can learn how to control it.'

He didn't say anything when she said things like that, but he didn't pull away from her, either, and she took that as a hopeful sign.

She was frowning at the rice and nudging a bit of it onto her spoon to check the seasonings, wondering testily why she persisted in staying in contact with her father when it didn't seem to matter to him, when Greg said suddenly, 'You don't like your father.'

It was one of his flat statements, sent up like a flag. He would never have asked her a question about something like that. She stopped with her spoon halfway to her mouth.

'That's not true.'

'You get upset every time he comes here. You yell at me a lot.'

Unaware that she yelled at him much at all – believing, in fact, that she was extraordinarily patient – Breanne scowled.

Before she could say anything, Greg was adding to his list of evidence, sounding like a miniature prosecuting attorney. 'When he's here you're all nervous. When he

16

leaves you're all quiet and sad. You don't like him.'

'I guess,' she said slowly, 'in a way you're right. I love my father, but most of the time I don't like him very much.'

'I don't know why,' Greg informed her. 'He's nice. You putting *cinnamon* in there?'

'A pinch of cinnamon, a dash of cloves, a little bit of curry,' she sang, then leaned over the stove toward him, put her hand on the back of his head, and kissed him. 'I love you.'

'I love you, too,' he said at once, as he had from the first day. She hurried to turn away so that he wouldn't see how much that meant to her, how afraid she was of reading too much into the words he said so easily.

But now she was thinking head-on about her father. She mixed the seasoned rice with the cooked chicken and the raisins and almonds, and put the casserole into the oven over Greg's objections that the temperature was too high. Then she went upstairs to change her clothes. She was nervous. Around her father she had always been nervous, and since her mother's death it was worse.

Her mother was dead. Standing by her dresser, holding a clean pair of jeans, Breanne gasped and doubled over in physical pain. It had been almost a year now, and still the loss was so enormous that it was almost incomprehensible. Her mother was dead. She'd never known her mother; her father had always been in the way.

'What's wrong with Daddy?' The question that framed and supported her childhood, the tension in their house, the thing that bound Breanne and her mother and her sister together when they would have had nothing in common, or when, without it, they would have been forced to discover something better. 'What's wrong with Daddy today?'

'He has a headache.' He always had a headache. She did not remember resenting it; she remembered, in fact, admiring his strength in the face of unimaginable pain. But Daddy's headaches, Daddy's moods, were the warp of her family life, and everybody had to take care of him.

17

'He has a headache.'

'He's mad about something. I don't know what.'

'He has a headache.'

'He's mad at me.'

Often he wouldn't speak to them for days, and they never would know exactly what was wrong, and his father's tension spread palpably throughout the house.

She had always been afraid to be alone with him, and throughout her childhood she had been alone with him a lot because it was a family myth that Breanne was Daddy's girl. She was afraid he would say something she couldn't understand, try to give her something she couldn't take. And, when she was a teenager and almost ready to leave home, almost ready to escape from him, it had happened.

They had been riding their bikes, the four of them, down the dirt road that encircled her parents' house. Breanne's mother and sister couldn't keep up and, suddenly, Breanne found herself alone with her father in a thick Pennsylvania woods, the trees green around them, the underbrush tangled. The sky was gray, the birds were singing furiously, and he was saying from out of the woods behind her, 'You know, I never wanted to get married.'

She'd said nothing, concentrating on negotiating the holes and rocks in the road, concentrating on avoiding the voice as it came at her like a poisoned arrow out of the green woods. Her breath was coming short and painfully.

'I wanted to be a musician and go on the road. I played a pretty mean alto sax in those days.'

'So why didn't you?'

She didn't know if he had heard her, and what she wanted to shout at him was, don't tell me this don't tell me anything like this I don't want to know.

'Your mother was in love with me. She needed me. She wanted to get married. I had just turned down another girl and I felt terrible about it. I didn't want to do it again. So I married your mother. I got a job at the post office. And then you came along. I never wanted to have a child, either, but then you came along and then Claire came along, and I stayed at the post office for thirty-one years until I retired.'

Breanne had never heard him say so much about himself, before or since. She knew she should be honored. What she felt instead was skin-crawling horror. Betrayal. Any other person she would have encouraged to tell her more, but this, after all, was her *father*. She swerved her bike too far to the right to avoid a pothole and fell in the dirt, scraping her elbow and bursting into tears.

That evening, she remembered, Daddy had had a terrible headache, and she had moved out of her parents' home as soon as she could.

Breanne stood still and barely breathing as the realisation swept over her; instead of escaping the anger and the love that felt like anger, she had trapped herself in the same house with it again. Scrupulously she had avoided falling in love with men like her father, and it had not always been easy; now here she was, adopting one for her son.

The doorbell rang. Breanne smoothed her hair and tucked in her shirt, distractedly wondering what parents saw when they looked at their adult children, and went downstairs. Greg had answered the door. She heard the low, halting sounds of the two of them talking, her father and her son, before she entered the room.

'I really don't see how we're going to get out of this mess we're in,' Andy said later over her chicken-and-rice casserole. 'This economy is the worst it's been since the Depression.'

'What's that mean?' Greg demanded, his eyes clearing slightly from the glazed look they'd had ever since Andy started talking. Relieved for the moment from having to design responses which would appear to show a willingness to 'discuss' without being in the least argumentative, Breanne retreated gratefully to the kitchen to fill the coffee cups. She listened, smiling, to her father's terse, impatient explanations of economic theory to Greg, whose questions were almost total *non sequiturs*.

When she came back to the table she saw Greg fussing

with the edge of her father's placemat, narrowing his eyes at the water glass, which tipped and swayed.

'Stop it, Greg,' she said sharply, interrupting her father in mid-sentence.

'Stop what?' Not looking at her, not moving his hand.

'If you don't stop it,' she told him evenly, 'you can leave the table.' He sighed heavily, glowered at her, and leaned on the table with his head on his hand.

There was a pause. Then Andy said, 'And nuclear war. I really don't see how we can avoid blowing ourselves up. Not that it matters, of course, in the scheme of things. I mean, human life isn't very important when you look at the whole universe. We can blow ourselves up, as I for one believe we will soon, and the universe won't even notice.'

'Oh, come on, Daddy,' Breanne protested, glancing protectively at Greg. She didn't want him growing up scared. She didn't want her father corrupting her son with titillating, self-satisfied pessimism. She didn't want to have to grow old wondering what was wrong with Greg. 'I don't think things are that bad. And anyway, you can't go through life worrying about things like nuclear war.'

'You don't think so?' Andy's eyes lit up. His voice quickened and sharpened in excitement. Trapped. Too late, Breanne saw that she'd given him whatever he was desperate for, and now he wouldn't stop talking about nuclear war for the rest of the evening. Though her hands were already shaking and her stomach acid, she poured herself another cup of coffee.

It was a school night, and Greg went to bed before Andy left. His bedroom was right off the living room and he could hear them talking, words and phrases running together as he fought sleep.

Nuclear war. The Bomb. Just thinking about it gave him the creeps. All that power. All that noise and light. Everybody dead, including him.

He draped a blanket over his lamp, turned the lamp on, and sat up in bed. Sooner or later she'd notice the light under his door and make him turn it off, but in the meantime he could play. The room was filled with strange, thick shadows cast by the red blanket over the lamp, and when he put his hand on it the flesh was red, too, the bones black.

Quietly Greg got out of bed and went to sit on the floor in the far corner of the room. He stared at the light. He thought about the Bomb. He imagined as clearly as he could the lamp blowing up, throwing red glass and white light everywhere, killing everybody, including him.

He thought about it hard, and the thought was nice. But he was sleepy. He wasn't mad enough, even at the stupid old man who was, incredibly, Breanne's father, but was for sure not his grandfather, would never be his grandfather. He couldn't do it. The lamp stayed put. The blanket glowed.

Finally Greg got back into bed, hid his face in the cool pillow and fell asleep.

5

Greg woke up at two o'clock in the morning, sweating, shaking with fury. Before he was even fully awake, his mind was roiling with red and black pictures of things cracking, shattering, blowing up, and he was afraid to open his eyes.

When he did, he didn't know where he was. The room was still weirdly lit in red. A dull-brown spot had appeared on the shade of the bedlamp and he could smell the faint odor of something burning. He switched off the lamp and then the room was dark and strange.

Through the rage which was threatening to drown him, Greg listened. He could hear the people in the house next door fighting again, the shouted exchange of bad words, the slammed doors. He could hear the occasional *rush* of a car down the street. He could hear a cat yowling somewhere to be let in. None of these sounds, identifiable as they were, helped him to know where he was. A part of his mind said that he was in his own bedroom in his own home, his adoptive home, his forever home, but that didn't make any sense and he couldn't place himself.

He lay in the darkness, panting, trembling. Inside his head formless things splattered into a million bloody pieces; those things, and the fury that flung and twisted them, were real. Houses, he thought he saw. Toys and dishes. Bones. Faces.

His mother's face.

He had been dreaming about his mother. His mother

was his dream. She lived inside his head and he was never free of her. He had lost her because he was bad.

'Mama.'

The face of his mother loomed whole and smiling behind his eyes. Greg opened his eyes and she was still there, smiling, saying she loved him. He felt her hands on him. He felt her surrounding him again, threatening to drown him, promising to keep him safe.

With all his strength Greg pushed his mother away, and watched with sick satisfaction as she broke and melted all over the place. Her blood drenched him; his tears were hot and red. He had killed his mother. Over and over again he had killed his mother, and she still kept coming back.

'Oh, Mama!'

Greg was crying. He grabbed the edge of his sheet with both hands and pulled hard in opposite directions, but it was almost brand new and it wouldn't rip. Blindly he reached up, pulled something from the shelf over his head, and threw it against the wall. But it was a heavy, black-metal sculpture of a horse, and it thudded without breaking.

He didn't understand this power he had. When he needed it most, it wouldn't come. He could break toys, sometimes, or other people's belongings; sometimes he could hurt people who were trying to hurt him. But at times like this, when he thought the anger that lived inside him was really going to eat him up or break him apart trying to get out, he was helpless. Sometimes, furiously, Greg doubted that he had any real power at all.

'Mama!' He was writhing on the bed. His stomach hurt and his head hurt and his arms and legs were tingling painfully. He gasped. He let his mouth gape and opened his eyes wide and spread his legs, anything he could think of to let the anger out before it killed him.

'*Mama!*' He was calling her now, screaming, though he couldn't be sure he was making any noise. He was sweating and shivering. '*Mama!*' Somebody had to come. Somebody had to take care of him. Somebody had to keep him safe. 'MAMA!'

Suddenly his own face leaped out of the darkness at him, his own body twisted and spun toward certain impact with something huge and hard that he couldn't see. Knowing what to expect, he waited for the pain and the blood. Maybe this time he would die.

But nothing happened. His face hung there, his body wrenched and splayed, and the rage built up like an avalanche, like a hurricane, like a bomb. Greg knew he was going to explode, there would be pieces of him everywhere, and still he would not be dead.

He leaped to his feet and tore out of the room. Hardly aware of what he was doing, he raced up the stairs to Breanne's room and pounded desperately on her door. 'Mama! Mama! I can't sleep!'

Breanne woke with a start out of a sound sleep and lay rigid in the dark, wondering what had awakened her. She heard the neighbors fighting again, a very young couple, but that was practically a nightly occurrence and she didn't think it would have disturbed her. She heard a cat yowling to be let in and wondered vaguely if it was one of her own. She heard the *rush* of tires on wet pavement and noted wearily that it was raining again.

A thud from downstairs made her sit up in bed. Something was wrong with Greg. She fumbled for her robe and slippers, listening hard, and heard nothing else. Maybe she hadn't heard anything, or only the noise made by the impatient cat thumping at the door.

She turned on the lamp beside her bed and shielded her eyes from its glare. Her mind was groggy and her head ached. She had been dreaming about her father – her father holding her, her father in an unreachable white tower up an impossible flight of circular stairs, her father dead. All frequent dream images for her – disturbing but familiar.

But there had been a new one, and she supposed that was the cause of her acute dismay, the strong sense of imminent disaster. The clearest image she had from this night's dream was her father's head exploding, showering her with his intimate red blood.

24

Breanne held her breath, pressed a fist over her heart as if to keep it quiet, and listened. Nothing. But she was wide awake now, and certain that something was wrong. She stood up and was heading for the stairs when the pounding came at her door and she heard the terrified wail: 'Mama! Mama! I can't sleep!'

As she rushed to him she acknowledged to herself with deep pleasure that for the first time he had called her Mama. She fell to her knees and took him in her arms, thinking how small he was for all his rapid growth. He was hot, probably feverish. He was shaking violently. He had been crying, though he wasn't crying now. He stood rigid in her arms, his hands at his sides, his face against her shoulder only because she pressed it there.

'Greg, sweetheart, what's wrong?'

'I can't sleep.'

'Are you sick?' She tried to feel his forehead but he turned his face into the soft lapel of her robe, so she put her hand on the back of his neck and found it wet with sweat.

'I just can't sleep.'

'Did you have a bad dream?'

But he wouldn't say any more. He just stood there, leaning slightly against her now, and she tightened her arms around him and rocked back and forth on her knees and made small crooning noises and kissed him. He relaxed a little. She thought he might even be falling asleep.

She stood up, her legs stiff, and led him by the hand down the stairs. 'Come on. I'll lie down with you awhile.'

He was too big for her to lift, but she helped him into bed and tucked the covers around him. He lay on his stomach and his face was turned toward the wall. She ran her hands over his back, massaging, caressing. She smoothed his dark hair and lightly touched his cheek. He was still hot, but his breathing was more regular now and he seemed to have stopped shaking.

Squinting, Breanne looked around his room. Amid the piles of clothes and comic books against the far wall was the dark shape of something he had thrown, which would account for the thud. She detected a burning odor, saw the faint outline of a scorched place on his lampshade, and made a mental note to take it away from him until he was ready to handle it safely. Otherwise, his room seemed unchanged, normal – except for her persistent feeling that something was wrong.

'I'm going to get a thermometer,' she whispered. 'I'll be right back.'

'Don't go!'

Breanne lay down and curled herself around him. She pulled him close and decided to play a hunch, take a chance. 'Were you thinking about Debbie?' That was the way she'd decided to refer to his birthmother, though she'd never mentioned the name to him before and wasn't sure he'd even recognise it.

He did. His body stiffened and she expected an angry denial or an emphatic silence. Instead, he admitted in a small, scared voice, 'Yes.'

'What were you thinking about her?'

But that was too much. After awhile he said, 'I don't know.'

Breanne hugged him. 'You miss her, don't you?'

At once this time. 'Yes.'

'It makes you sad that you can't be with her.'

'Yes. And – ' He struggled. 'And mad. Real mad.'

She kissed his hair. 'You'll probably feel like that for a long time. You love her and you hate her, both.' He said nothing. Carefully, she said, 'I'm your mother now. But I'll never take Debbie's place in your heart any more than she can take mine. You can love us – and maybe hate us – both.'

He didn't say anything. She couldn't guess what he had heard, what he had understood. But he snuggled back against her then and, like the small child he was, abruptly fell asleep.

Breanne lay with him for awhile, comforted and touched by her child in her arms, but also profoundly uneasy. There as something in the air, something in the room with them. A tension. A presence. She shivered, withdrew her arm gently, and left Greg's room. She left the door slightly ajar – so she could hear him if he called her again, but also, she knew, to provide a way out for whatever was in that room.

For a few moments she stood in the doorway, listening, watching him, but there was nothing. Then, as quietly as she could, she went back upstairs to her own bed and, she guessed, to her own throbbing dreams.

Andy couldn't sleep. He had awakened at two o'clock in the morning with a severe headache, and now, though some of the pain had seeped away, it was well after three and he still couldn't get back to sleep.

He had switched on the radio almost as soon as he'd came awake, its dial always set to the twenty-four-hour talk radio station because that was the only thing on the air worth listening to. The voices hummed in his dark room like crickets, vaguely annoying, vaguely pleasant. Over the years Andy had learned to keep the volume down so that Ruth could sleep, although privately he was convinced that she could sleep through anything. The cup of tea on his bedside stand was cold but he sipped at it anyway, grimly. Ruth had always hoped that herbal tea would help his headaches.

He missed her. Bitterly he missed her, and tears welled up in his eyes. Furiously rubbing them away, he sat up in bed and turned on the light. On the yellow legal pad he always kept on the stand, he began to make careful notes, preparing for his nightly call to the all-night talk-show host. Tonight the topic was nuclear disarmament, and he had a few things to say about that.

Sudden pain shot up his neck and circled his head. And gasped for breath. At the same time he was thinking about the boy, about the anger in the boy's brown eyes.

He felt himself to be in danger. Breanne was in danger and, agonised, Andy knew he would split apart like powdery old wood if anything happened to her. The light assaulted his eyes. He turned it out and reached for the phone. It was all he could do not to call Breanne.

Instead he dialed, without looking, the call-in number of the radio station. The bright-voiced young woman who always answered the phone answered tonight. 'Good morning. This is *The Karen Mallory Show*. Would you like to speak with Karen on the air?'

'Yes,' he said, gruffly. He cleared his throat and tried again. 'Yes. I would.'

'Oh, hi, Andy.'

It embarrassed him that she knew his voice. He did not like to think of himself as one of the lonely insomniacs who called in regularly to all-night talk shows in order to say what they couldn't say to anybody else.

'What would you like to talk to Karen about this morning?'

'Nuclear disarmament,' he informed her curtly.

'Okay,' the producer said brightly. 'There are two calls ahead of you, Andy, and then you'll be on the air.'

She put him on hold. He waited, hearing a faint, rhythmic sound over the telephone wire that he could imagine to be his own heartbeat. That old heart wouldn't be beating much longer. The thought of his own death didn't frighten him, though he believed there was no life after this one, fervently believed there was no god. Yet tonight, sitting alone in his house waiting to talk to a young woman he had never met, whose face he did not even visualise when he talked to her, whose name he barely remembered from one week to the next – tonight Andy Novak was visited by a searing apprehension of his own mortality, and his mother's, and his daughter's, and that of this dangerous young boy, and his head seemed about to burst.

6

School wasn't bad. Whenever anybody asked him about school – and grownups were always asking him about school because they didn't know what else to talk to him about – Greg shrugged and did his best to look disgusted, but it really wasn't that bad. Whenever he woke up with a sore throat or a headache, Breanne let him stay home without a hassle, and he knew he could get away with faking it, but he never did.

His grades were okay. Not brilliant, but okay. He did what he had to do to get by, and in geography, for instance, he got a B when they had to draw all the flags of all the countries in the world, bright colors and neat, straight lines. Some of his foster parents had really had a thing about grades, as if those Cs and Ds and Fs had belonged to them instead of to him. Mr Ortega had promised a dollar for every A and a paddling for every F, and Greg had never once collected either. It had been a matter of pride.

At school Greg got into fights sometimes. Sometimes he got sent to the principal's office. On parents' night he always knew what they were going to say about him. This year he was the teacher's right-hand man. He had been moved up there by the teacher's desk, away from the other kids. That was fine by him, no matter how much they teased him. It was safer there. Something in him also liked being separated from the other kids, set apart.

'Greg,' the teacher would sometimes say, 'you're driving

me crazy.' Or, 'Greg, I'm not putting up with this today.'
And once even, 'You know something, Greg? I don't like
you very much today.'

That had hurt. Greg had cried. At first he didn't think
Mr Franconi had seen him. He stared straight ahead at the
decimal problem on the blackboard, and a long piece of
yellow chalk snapped in the tray and bounced onto the
floor. Mr Franconi glanced at the chalk on the floor, but
he was so mad at Greg and so preoccupied with trying to
teach the decimal problem that he didn't do anything
about it. Greg waited, not knowing what was going to
happen. At recess Mr Franconi kept him in and they
talked, and Greg ended up crying again and saying, 'I
don't know why I do the things I do. I think something's
really wrong with me.' Then he waited, anxiously, to see
how much more he dared tell this kind man.

'Nothing's wrong with you.' The teacher put his arm
around Greg's shoulders and that felt nice, even though
Greg already knew from that one sentence that he couldn't
tell his terrible secret to Mr Franconi, couldn't tell him
anything about the monstrous life-giving anger that lived
inside him like something from a horror movie or a fairy
tale he should have outgrown a long time ago. 'You just
have a lot going on inside you,' Mr Franconi said, 'and
you haven't learned how to control it yet. Nothing's
wrong with you that isn't wrong with the rest of us when
we're trying to grow up.'

You don't know, Greg thought desperately. You just
don't know. It wasn't like this for you. For some reason he
was thinking about Sherry, her round little face staring up
at him from her bed after something bad had happened to
him, her brown eyes telling him she understood maybe
better than he did what was going on.

His favorite teacher was Mrs Marx, in second grade. He
liked her so much that he flunked second grade on purpose,
so he could have her again. But by then he was in another
school so it didn't work. He should have known. He was a
dumb kid.

'You're crazy, man!' Pete was shouting gleefully at

Cameron. Cameron kept insisting that the Bears were going to win tonight against Wichita, when everybody knew they didn't stand a chance. Who gave a crap about the minors anyway? Greg sniffed and walked far ahead of the others.

Friends? He had plenty of friends. Almost every day he walked home from school with his friends. Pete and Cameron and Joel and Carl and Larry. Sometimes he even got into trouble with Breanne when he didn't come straight home, when he stopped without telling her to jump on Joel's tramp or play Cameron's Atari. Sometimes they came to his house, but not often. Breanne didn't say anything, but he knew she'd like it if he invited his friends over more often, and that was one of the reasons he didn't.

Friends? He had friends. Years of moving around with Debbie and living in foster homes had taught him how people come and go in your life, and that was fine with him. He could remember some of the kids he'd been in foster care with – kids the foster moms had insisted on calling his 'brothers' and 'sisters' though he'd had only one sister and they'd taken her away from him because he was bad. He never wondered what had happened to any of those kids, and these were all the friends he needed.

Debbie. It still felt weird thinking her name. He'd been in his first foster home before it dawned on him that she had a name other than Mommy. He was a dumb kid. Now most of the time when he thought about her it was Debbie. Debbie. He knew girls named Debbie. Sometimes just thinking her name, or Sherry's, could make him mad.

'Hey, Greg. Comin' to the game with us?'

'Nah, Breanne won't let me.'

That wasn't true, of course. She'd love to see him doing things with his friends. She didn't think he had enough friends. But all of a sudden he'd had enough of these guys, his *friends*. He could take only so much friendship. He scowled.

'What a dumb name. Bree-anne.' Carl drew the name out long and curled his mouth around it so it really did sound dumb. Greg hated it, and quickly tried to fill his mind with something other than the pleasant thought of Carl's head exploding. His mind was heating up dangerously.

'How come you call her that, anyway?' Larry demanded.

'Why not, fucker? It's her name.'

'Hey, Novak, is she your *real* mom?'

'Go fuck yourself,' Greg said, and ran across the street to his house. When he first came to live here, he and Breanne and the social worker had practiced what to say when somebody asked him stuff like that, everything from 'I'm adopted' straight out to 'She's as real as they come.' It all sounded stupid to Greg.

Sometimes when he wasn't with her, he didn't believe in Breanne. Sometimes Debbie and Sherry and the shadowy hurting men were more real than she was. It was weird. It made him feel weird about himself. It was her fault. He shook his head angrily.

He walked around the house for a little while, feeling its emptiness. Maybe she wasn't coming home. The Ortegas had gone away on vacation without him and while they were gone they decided they didn't want him anymore, and so he just never saw them again. He'd lived with them over a year. But he didn't really believe that would happen this time. He didn't really believe she was like everybody else. Loss of that belief was itself a loss, and it made him mad.

He sat down at the dining-room table and pulled a blue ballpoint pen and his Big Chief tablet out of his school bag. 'Dear Mrs Marx,' he wrote, remembering after all this time how to spell her name. It wasn't 'Marks'. He'd worked hard on that. Mrs Marx had said he was a smart boy. 'I'm adopted,' he wrote, and paused. He couldn't think what else to say. Frowning, the letters going all slanted and wobbly, he added, 'How are you? I am fine,' and signed his name: 'Greg Novak.'

'Dummy,' he said aloud to himself. She wouldn't know who he was by that name. Underneath his signature he wrote – clumsily, for it had been a long time – his old name: Thurber.

He got an envelope out of the drawer, put his letter

inside, and sealed it. In the phone book he found an address for a Gwendolyn Marx and knew that had to be her, though he'd never consciously thought of her having a first name, either. Painstakingly, tongue between his teeth, he addressed the envelope.

Then he realised he'd have to ask Breanne for a stamp. He knew she'd give it to him without any questions – she was always talking about privacy – but the thought of even having to ask enraged him. He pounded his fist on the table and tossed the envelope across the room. While it was in the air, he tried to make it disintegrate into a shower of tiny white flakes, but it was too soft, too floating, and it got away from him to drift to the floor intact.

Greg slammed out of the house and unlocked his bike from the porch railing with such force that the wrought iron sang. He sped down the sidewalk and into the street, going against the traffic and flipping off the first honking car that came toward him.

It was late that afternoon when he left the Boys' Club, and he knew the minute he stepped out the door that something was wrong. The air felt different – alive, angry, charged with electricity. He looked toward the mountains and saw that the western sky was filled with clouds of a weird gray color, tinged around the edges with yellow the color of pus. Something was going to happen. Something was going to explode. He could feel it in his head.

He had trouble unlocking his bike. Again and again he tried, but the padlock wouldn't budge. Around him the wind had started, like a voice, like a knife. It whirled and spat gravel against his legs. He breathed deeply and managed to calm himself enough to try the combination one more time, slowly. When the lock gave he found himself almost in tears.

He got on his bike and started home. There didn't seem to be anybody else on the street. The air was hot in his lungs, charged with an eerie power. He stood up off the seat and pedaled hard. Rain had started now, hard drops needling his face, injecting him with a strange excitement.

He sped through intersections without looking for cars, and there didn't seem to be any anywhere.

Then the siren started. Greg knew at once it was an air-raid siren; he'd never heard one before, but he'd seen the movies. The Bomb. The nuclear bomb. Crazily, he thought of Andy, the old man's jaw always set so hard it was no wonder he had headaches, and hoped he was having a bitch of a headache now.

He rode his bike furiously through the black streets and the black wail of the siren, and there was no one there. Mama, he thought, and the tears started. He was going to die, and he didn't want to die alone. In his fear and fury, and because in this strange light everything looked different, he took a wrong turn and ended up going two blocks out of his way, the panic rising in him like blood.

Finally he saw it – his own house. The wind was so strong by now that he could hardly stay on his bike. The black-and-yellow clouds had spread over the whole sky. The siren kept on; he couldn't even think around its shrill monotone. But he saw his own house, up in the next block on the right. He hunched over the handlebars and pedaled as fast as he could, certain he wouldn't make it before the Bomb fell.

If he made it home, she would be there. His real mother, the one who was there to take care of him. She would protect him. If he could just make it home. The bike skidded on the wet pavement and he almost fell.

Abruptly Greg imagined the Bomb hurtling toward him out of the black sky, and wondered if his power could stop it. He pulled over to the curb and shut his eyes hard, visualising a huge metal object hard and hollow inside, willing it to explode in his head. In his mind the thing blew up a dozen times, and the shards of metal and mushroom of white gas flew all over inside him, making him wince and cry out. But when he opened his eyes he could see that it hadn't worked. The siren was still going, the sky was still black and yellow, the wind was still rising, and he had had no effect at all.

He kicked frantically to get his bike started up the hill to his house. He glanced over his shoulder at the mountains again and realised in a rush what it really was. The funnel cloud separated from the heavy gray bank of clouds and hung obscenely against the putrid yellow sky. It was not the Bomb. It was not the end of the world. It was a tornado, and he could be killed, or picked up and carried away to some scary place, but he did not have to keep it from blowing up the world.

Rain was coming at him in sheets when he finally reached the porch. He let the bike fall over on its side and dashed to the door, wanting more than anything to be inside, where he and Breanne could wait out the storm together. He pulled hard on the door handle. The door was locked.

It must be earlier than he'd thought. Breanne wasn't home from work yet. He'd slammed the door when he left and hadn't thought to bring his key. He could hear the phone ringing inside the house. He could see through the front window the warm lamp on and the white cat asleep on the back of the couch. But he couldn't get in. He was alone, locked out in the middle of a tornado.

Slowly Greg turned to face the storm. He was afraid, and terribly excited. Rain cut in under the porch roof and left sharp tracks on the concrete. Shingles and branches tumbled into the yard. He pressed his back against the brick wall of the house and tried to open himself to the storm, to take from it whatever power it had before it forced its way inside. The air-raid siren howled.

7

Breanne was going *out*. Going out with a *man*. Greg couldn't believe it. She'd gone out before – for an hour or two, once for the whole evening – but it had always been with women. He'd met those women, looked at them, and he knew she'd never leave him for somebody like that.

This was different. She was going out with a man. Somebody named Jeff whom Greg had never heard of. They were going on a date, to dinner and a play. Greg had never been to a play. It was a stupid play that Breanne said he wouldn't like, and she was probably right about that. It was called *The Caucasian Chalk Circle* and sounded like school. A stupid fucking *man* he'd never heard of. She was going to pick him up so Greg wouldn't even get to meet him, fix his face in his mind.

The worst part was she was leaving him with Andy, that stupid old man. Greg was almost twelve years old and he didn't need a babysitter. Breanne said it was against the law, it was child neglect, to leave a child under twelve alone. He was no child.

She was taking a bath. He could hear the water running. Running and running. She always used up all the hot water and the bathroom was always steamy and smelled like flowers when she was done. It made Greg sick.

He went into his room and slammed a few things around. He was allowed to break anything that belonged to him, anything in his room except the door and the window, and he almost had. The other night when she'd sent him to his room for not letting her know he'd gone to the Boys' Club – the night they'd almost had a tornado and then, to his intense discomfort, had not – he'd thrown every single one of his collection of bottles against the wall. Thinking about it now, he couldn't be sure if he'd done it with his hands or with his mind. Sometimes the two seemed the same to him anyway.

He picked up his baseball bat and brought it down hard on the top of his dresser, which Breanne had painted bright red for him before he came. The wood splintered nicely and the red paint came off in chunks. He smashed the dresser until it lay in pieces at his feet. That helped some. He was panting and his shoulders ached. But she was still going out without him tonight. Going out with a *man*.

Greg threw the bat across his bed, where it bounced harmlessly and rolled against his headboard. He stood there for a minute with his fists clenched at his sides, then softly opened the door. He could hear her in the bathroom, splashing and singing. *Singing.* He scowled. Walking on tiptoe, he crept to the bathroom door.

The door was old, like the rest of the house. Most of the time Greg disdained anything older than he was; he liked to point out approvingly to Breanne those treeless new housing developments that she hated. But now the age of the house worked to his advantage. Long ago somebody had fitted the bathroom door with a knob way too small for it, so that above the knob was a half-circle gap of about a quarter of an inch at its widest point, a hole in the door you could see through. Greg was sure that Breanne didn't know it was there.

He held his breath, crouched, and peered through the hole. He could see her. She was standing up in the tub, and she was naked.

The clock struck the half-hour and Greg jumped. He took his eye away from the hole and let out his breath in a slow, soundless gasp, thinking for sure his chest would burst before he could get all the air out. She was naked in there. He could see her. She wasn't really his mother.

He crouched and peered again. She was looking at herself in the full-length mirror on the other side of the door; that, he realised, was why she seemed to be looking right at him, meeting his gaze. But still Greg wondered crazily if she knew what he was doing. It wouldn't be the first time she'd known something he would have sworn she couldn't know – it happened so often, in fact, that sometimes he caught himself wondering if she had some kind of special power, too.

Greg silently shifted position. He was getting a hard-on. She turned this way and that, lifted her arms over her head, cupped her hands under her breasts. If he wanted to he could break the door down, just by thinking about it. The thought excited and horrified him. His penis rose.

Then, as Breanne lifted one leg and stepped – dripping, shining – out of the tub, he moved quickly away from his watching place and hurried back to his room. He shut the door and lay on his bed. His penis throbbed – not altogether unpleasantly, but with such insistence that he couldn't lie still. He put a picture in his mind of whatever was inside his penis spurting out and the pressure easing away, but nothing happened. Stealthily, he put one hand there, while the other hand curled into a fist by his cheek.

It was Breanne's first date in over a year. In all that time she had met maybe half a dozen interesting men: three of them had been married, one had been gay, and the other two were obviously not interested in her. Jeff was an old friend. They'd graduated together from business school years ago, had dated now and then, and she'd scarcely missed him when he moved away.

When he called to say he was in town for a few days she'd happily accepted his dinner invitation, and only after she hung up did she start worrying about leaving Greg.

To her surprise – considering how sexually active she'd been throughout college and graduate school and shortly thereafter – Breanne had not much missed men. As quickly as her desire for motherhood had come upon her, so, it seemed, her desire for romance and sex had departed.

The desire – the determination – to be a mother had come upon her almost literally overnight. Always she had hedged about having children, shuddered at the thought of pregnancy and childbirth, cringed at the idea of a lifelong commitment like that. For a long time, having discovered no maternal instinct in herself at all, she had thought she probably would never have kids, and had resigned herself, sadly but also with relief, to that choice.

Then one morning she woke up and it was there – the need elaborated, the decision made. It was as if, unknown to her conscious mind, she had been working the problem as the sculptor works clay, and she knew what to do. That morning she called Social Services and began the process of applying for adoption, and an appropriate nine months later she brought Greg home.

Greg. She realised that one of the things she was most looking forward to tonight was the chance to tell Jeff about Greg. She stretched in the hot water, listened to the silence from the rest of the house, and shook her head. Apparently smashing his furniture, or whatever he'd been doing in there, had made him feel better about her going out. It was hard for her when he was that angry, especially at her. She had to leave the living room when he was breaking things on the other side of the wall, so that she wouldn't rush in and stop him.

She gave herself a final rinse, pulled the plug, and stood up in the tub. A mirror hung on the inside of the door and she looked at herself critically, raised her arms above her head, cupped her hands under her breasts. Not bad. She'd always liked the way she looked. Not like the centerfolds in the *Playboy*s and *Penthouse*s Greg had started sneaking into the house, but not bad.

She climbed out of the tub and toweled herself dry, taking her time, enjoying the sensation of getting ready for a date. Hearing the clock strike the half-hour, she calculated that in forty-five minutes or so she'd have to leave to pick up Jeff at his motel. That left time to get her father and son settled down to dinner. The thought of them spending the entire evening together alone brought a hard little knot of anxiety back to her throat, but she shook her head, swallowed, and made it go away. Their relationship was their responsibility, not hers.

Anyway, the lunar eclipse was tonight. She couldn't have done better if she'd planned it herself. Her father had always loved to lecture her about astronomy, and Greg had a nascent interest. They should have plenty of safe things to talk about while she was gone.

She listened again for noise from Greg and, hearing none, turned the hair dryer on high.

'That shirt doesn't look at all good on you,' Greg observed when she came into the living room a few minutes later. He'd barely looked up from his *Sports Illustrated*. Her father would be here any minute.

'Thanks,' Breanne said, and then despite herself went to look in the mirror. Actually, she thought, she looked good tonight. The white scooped-neck shirt made her slight tan seem darker than it was, and the black pants fitted with just the right degree of snugness. Her hair looked full and nearly as dark as Greg's. She smiled at her reflection, stuck her tongue out at Greg, adjusted the thin gold chain around her neck, and went to check on dinner.

'Well,' said Andy finally as the two of them sat across from each other eating chili. Greg loved chili and he knew that was why Breanne had made it tonight. That made him mad, and he'd meant not to eat very much of it, but he was already on his third bowlful. The old man started again: 'Are we going to watch the eclipse tonight?'

Automatically Greg said, 'Huh?' although he had heard. He knew that habit of his drove grownups crazy. He didn't do it on purpose to bug them, but it didn't bother him that it bugged them either.

Andy sighed and repeated, 'Are we going to watch the eclipse tonight?'

'What's that?' Greg asked, although he knew vaguely.

'A lunar eclipse. An eclipse of the moon,' Andy said. 'The earth's shadow covers the moon. Tonight's eclipse is supposed to be spectacular because of all the volcanic ash in the air.'

'What makes an eclipse?' It astonished Greg to find himself both genuinely curious and actually looking to the old man for answers to something he wanted to know.

Andy cleared his throat and began a detailed explanation of eclipses and other heavenly phenomena. It was his lecture voice.

After supper they left the dishes and went out and sat on the back steps, the two of them together, and Greg saw bushy clouds moving in over the mountains. 'It's gonna rain,' he said flatly. 'There ain't gonna be no eclipse.' He saw Andy wince at his grammar and grinned.

'It'll clear off,' Andy said in the same flat tone.

Greg thought about snapping back, 'Wishful thinking,' or, 'That's all *you* know about it,' but he stopped himself in time.

He could tell the old man was counting on this stupid eclipse. He could guess what he was thinking: The two of them watching the eclipse together, finding something in common. The image pleased Greg, too, and he began to be pissed off.

He glared at the old man. 'I bet you don't know shit about eclipses,' he said, more loudly than he'd meant to.

Andy's head snapped around and the hard little eyes fixed on him, reflecting the sunset like moons themselves. *Eclipse*, thought Greg savagely. *I'd like to eclipse you, you old bastard*. Frightened, he stopped the thought.

It was hours before the eclipse was supposed to start, and Greg didn't know what to do with himself. He wished Breanne were home. She was out with that man. He lay in the middle of the living-room floor with the stereo headphones on, hating the confinement of them against his ears, hating the silent old man who sat in the same room with him, watching some dumb show about the stock market on educational TV.

Andy hadn't talked to him anymore after he'd finished his lecture about eclipses. Greg couldn't think of any more questions. Andy disapproved of him. His disapproval stalked them like a living creature, between them like

Greg's own anger. Greg thought of his anger in colors like red and orange and purple and exploding black, in motion like the cars at the Indy 500, avoiding the wall by a hair. He thought of Andy's disapproval as thick, stagnant brown water, smelling like shit and oil, smelling the way a body and a machine would smell after they had hit the wall.

Dinner was wonderful, at an exquisite little French restaurant Breanne had not known existed, though it wasn't far from her house. The play touched her. Jeff was delightful – easier to talk to than she remembered, warmer and far more interesting. His hair had receded a little and his beard was trimmed shorter, but otherwise he looked the same. Still, she wondered if she would have recognised him on the street. It was a pleasant combination of novelty and familiarity. Breanne was having a very good time.

'I wonder how Daddy and Greg are doing,' she said in the car. All night she had sternly resisted the impulse to call home.

'Don't they get along?'

'I don't know. Sometimes I think there's actually something special between them, but that's probably wishful thinking. Both of them can be difficult. Greg was furious with me for going out with you tonight.'

Jeff laughed pleasantly. She glanced at him and noted the oncoming headlights playing on his face and neck.

'He's jealous. I don't blame him. I'd be jealous of a beautiful brand-new mother, too.'

'Thank you,' Breanne said.

They were headed toward her house and she didn't want the evening to end. She peered out of the window and could not see the moon. For some reason she did not want to get home until the eclipse was over. Tomorrow Jeff would go back to Houston and it would be a long time before she ever saw him again. She stopped for a red light, feeling sad.

Jeff said quietly, 'Why don't you come up to my room for a drink? I'm not ready for this evening to end.'

By nine o'clock the sky was completely overcast. The city lights reflected a dim blood-red off the clouds. Pollution, Greg thought viciously. 'No eclipse tonight,' he told Andy again during a commercial.

'There will be an eclipse,' Andy corrected him. 'We just may not be able to see it.'

Son-of-a-bitch, Greg thought, and stormed outside, away from this old man who was supposed to be his grandfather and who wouldn't talk to him, didn't like him, wanted him to go away. Greg slammed the door. Then he waited with clenched fists for Andy to come after him, scolding, but he didn't.

Greg stomped up the back stairway, making as much noise as he could, making the old wooden steps quiver until, he hoped, they might break. The anger was leaping inside him, faster than the speed of light. It takes seven minutes for the light of the sun to get here. How long does it take for anger to get where it's going, old man? Sensing that Andy would know the answer to that one, too, and would keep it from him, Greg longed to give in to the anger, to lie down on the splintery landing and kick his legs and scream from the pit of his stomach and roll down the steps and hit his head and gouge his eyes out on a nail and land, bloody and howling, in the old man's lap.

He drew his knees up to his chin and glared at the sky. Behind the gray and purple clouds he could see a faint bloody glow where the moon was. He narrowed his eyes and held his breath and the anger was like a knife, flashing faster than the speed of light, and suddenly there was a rent in the clouds.

'Andy,' breathed Greg, but his voice was so low that the old man inside the house couldn't possibly have heard.

His head pounded. He rocked back and forth. He fought to keep the anger thin and sharp, and he thrust it as hard and as far as he could, and the clouds tore away from the moon. In the lower left-hand corner you could see the shadow of the earth, the shadow of the very place where he, Greg, was sitting now. The edge of the moon seemed to pulsate red and purple and orange. Greg clenched his teeth and held his breath.

Below him on a lower step stood Andy. Greg hadn't seen him come out, and he didn't dare take his eyes away from the clouds to look at him now. But he clearly saw the old man's form, and his face edged by light from the emerging moon, red as if it were a heart. Andy was staring at him, and suddenly Greg was sure he knew what he was doing.

Relief so immense flooded through him that he almost let the anger get away. This old man knew about the power because he had it himself – or had had it when he was young and lost it somehow. Greg had found one of his own kind. He had found a friend. And, fittingly, Andy was there to witness the first time Greg had tried to use the anger not to hurt somebody, not to break things, but to give the world a gift. Now, for the first time in his life, he would not be alone.

Greg wrapped his arms around himself to hold himself together while slowly, agonisingly, the clouds pulled away from the moon. He waited for Andy to say something, a benediction, though he did not know the word.

The earth's shadow was clear as a toothmark on the lower left-hand edge of the moon when Andy whispered hoarsely, 'You'll regret this, boy. You'll regret it as long as you live,' and disappeared back into the house.

8

They were sitting on the floor in front of the fireplace putting pictures of their first four months together into a brand-new photo album. Outside it was snowing hard. Greg could see car lights on the sheets of white flakes.

'Look,' said Breanne, smiling. 'Pictures of your birthday.'

He looked, and as always felt weird at the sight of his own face, caught forever – and, it seemed to him, forever wrongly – on the scrap of shiny paper. 'Big deal,' he said.

It had been a nice evening. She had made spaghetti for him and he'd helped her, testing the pasta, melting the butter for the garlic bread. She'd asked about school, as she usually did, and this time he'd told her things. About the science project and Jason's new adopted Korean sister and the school play next week – not the most important things that were happening to him, not the most private things, but close enough. Close enough to please her, he saw. Close enough to scare him. He liked the closeness as much as she did, and that was beginning to make him mad.

She was pushing too hard. This thing with the stupid pictures was too much, though when she'd suggested they put the pictures into the album tonight he'd thought it sounded okay. She thought she was hot shit. She thought she was his fucking mother.

He grabbed half a dozen pictures from her hand, not quite tearing them but bending the corners, and stuck them haphazardly onto a page. There were too many of them; they were crowded and crooked, and the plastic sheet over them had fat rows of air bubbles.

'There,' he said, and grinned at her.

'That won't do.' She took out a few of the pictures, straightened the rest, and smoothed the plastic over them. 'There.'

'That looks stupid.'

'I don't think so.'

'Well, then you're stupid, too.'

She looked at him. 'What's the matter, Greg? You're awfully cranky tonight. Is something bothering you?'

'I'm not cranky. You're the one who's cranky.'

'Well,' she said, still looking at him, 'maybe tonight's not the night to do this together.'

'Maybe not,' he said, and added conversationally, 'you mother-fucking bitch.'

Her face paled. She leaned across the photo album and grabbed his shoulders hard, trying to turn him over to spank him. He knew that's what she was trying to do; she'd done it once before and he'd let her, got him over her knee and actually spanked him hard five or six times. It was so unlike the other physical punishments he'd had in his life – the belts, the sticks, the rubber bands, the burning cigarettes – that it had taken him that long to realise what was going on. But then the spanking began to sting and he'd twisted away from her. She'd left him alone in his room then, both of them panting, both of them in tears. She'd made him stay in there a long time and sometimes he hadn't been able to hear any movement in the rest of the house and he thought maybe she'd left, until, grim-faced and speaking to him no more than she had to, she'd brought in his supper.

That wasn't going to happen this time. He was bigger now and he knew a helluva lot more about fighting than she did. He braced his hands against the chair behind him and kicked out at her with his knee, connecting with the soft part of her stomach.

She slapped him then, once, twice across his face, and he

thought he saw his blood on her hand where his nose was bleeding. Rage drenched him, poured through him in red-hot streams, and, though he lay well away from her, flat on his back and roaring, Breanne clutched at her throat. Her eyes widened, widened, as if they would pop out of her head, and he knew he could make them do that, and for an instant he imagined in perfect detail her blood, her pain, her blindness, and the image was so good and so clear that he was almost convinced he had already made it happen.

Then he stopped it. With a terrible effort, a thundering pain in his head and chest and groin, he brought the anger back inside himself, curled up around it, and howled. It was the first time he'd ever done that, the first time he'd ever kept the anger from hurting someone who was hurting him. He didn't understand why he'd done that now. He hated her. She thought she was his fucking mother.

Breanne was crying. Her hands were pressed to her temples and she was rocking back and forth on her knees. He had made her cry.

'Greg, Greg, you break my heart when you act like this.'

Harshly he managed to tell her, 'That's what I meant to do. Break your fucking heart,' and as soon as he had said it he knew it was true – physically, literally, a yearning for her blood and still-throbbing tissue to go flying all over the place.

She was shaking. She got to her feet and walked away from him. He was sure she would leave him now and he would never see her again, and part of him was relieved. Her back to him, she ordered, 'Go to your room.'

He went, sobbing violently. The dark little room was filled with piles of his broken things, his own things, and it was welcoming and safe. He threw himself face down on the bed in the dark and tried to calm himself, gulping at the air, balling his fists on the rumpled and torn bedspread as he consciously tried to slow his heart and wipe the terrible pictures out of his mind. Underneath the terror and pain and the red-hot presence of his anger was a kind of amazement at what he had done, a kind of pride.

He had not hurt her. He had not killed her, and he knew he could have. It had never before occurred to him to try to control his anger that way, and the discovery that he could do it excited him deeply.

He wondered if his mother knew how close they had come tonight to real violence between them, and decided that she probably did. As his own sobbing quieted and his heart stopped pounding in his ears, he could hear her in another part of the house. She was crying in a way he had never heard before, great rasping noises that sounded as if they would tear her apart.

He wanted to go to her. He wanted to say he was sorry. He wanted her to hold him and make it safe for him and tell him she would never leave. He wanted to tell him about his anger and the things it could do, and about his new-found power over it. He wanted her to know he could make eclipses happen for the whole world to see.

But he didn't dare. Instead he rolled onto his back and stared into the blackness of his room. Then he unzipped his pants, pulled out his hardening penis, and began frantically to masturbate.

9

Breanne was reading Greg a story. He was too old for bedtime stories and so they didn't call it that anymore, but he lay on the floor at her feet with his head against her ankles and his eyes closed, his dark hair startling against the bright yellows and blues of his quilt, and listened raptly to the Narnia books, which Breanne had been sure he would not like when he picked them out at the library. She herself found C. S. Lewis a little precious and pompous and more than a little sexist, but she was willing to read for the sheer pleasure of the language, for the beauty of the children's adventures as they escaped the plodding grownup world, and, most of all, for Greg's rare ease with her and with the book.

Even her father sat still, as though he might be paying attention. He did not approve of fantasy, and she'd thought he would leave the room or turn on the TV or decide it was time for him to go home. Greg was sometimes embarrassed and therefore sullen when there was closeness between them for outsiders to see – and Andy was most definitely an outsider to them both. She'd expected Greg to refuse her offer of a story tonight. Instead, he'd brought the book to her before she asked. The three of them sat together amid the comfortable reds and browns of the living room, the funnel of the lamplight and the glow of the coals keeping them safe with each other. It was Christmas Eve.

'They stood on cool green grass,' she read, 'sprinkled

with daisies and buttercups. A little way off along the riverbank, willows were growing. On the other side, tangles of flowering currant, lilac, wild rose, and rhododendron closed them in. The horse was tearing up delicious mouthfuls of new grass.

'All this time the Lion's song and his stately prowl to and fro, backwards and forwards, was going on.'

Breanne's mind wandered as she read. All of Greg's presents were wrapped and hidden under her bed. With pleasure she thought about the watch. He'd be delighted and she could hardly wait to see his face when he opened it, although she knew the watch would be permanently disassembled within a week. Her father's gifts still had to be wrapped. She'd been putting that off because she was unsure of them, the way she'd always been.

Her father went out of his way to hate Christmas, which was Breanne's favorite holiday. This Christmas, the first since her mother had died, he looked as if he meant it. Breanne missed her mother sharply. She'd had to make *kolachy* by herself this year, and the first batch had come out of the oven flattened and scorched and practically unrecognisable.

Reading some more about the golden lion Aslan who would save all those who believed in Him, Breanne wished she believed. She wished her mother were here. Her mother would love Greg, and would tell her what to do.

' "Well done," said Aslan, in a voice that made the earth shake.'

Melinda had listened to her account of the terrible fight with Greg last week and had not told her what to do. 'It does not,' she'd said, 'mean that Greg's a bad kid. Or that you're a bad mother.'

Breanne had looked up at her, laughing a little, on the verge of tears. 'It doesn't?'

'No. It doesn't. Virtually every family I know has incidents like that when their kids are adolescents. Nobody enjoys it, and it's not something you want to have happen every day, but it's normal. Especially with older adopted kids. Especially when they start to really get close. Closeness scares them to death.'

'It didn't seem to me that he was scared.' Breanne had shivered. 'What I felt from him was anger. Directed anger.'

Melinda had nodded, and Breanne had been struck again by the steadiness of this woman, the professional sureness. Sometimes it offended her that Melinda knew her job so well, but on balance it was an enormous relief. She had never dreamed that being a parent would be so hard.

'I told you,' Melinda had said, 'that he wouldn't be easy. Greg has a lot of anger from a lot of years and now, with you, it's beginning to look safe to let it out. I expect things to get worse before they get better.'

'I don't know,' Breanne had replied slowly, 'if I really *can* make it safe for him.'

Melinda had glanced at her sharply. 'Are you considering disruption?'

'No!' Breanne had been astounded, and unnerved by the sudden blunt reminder that Greg was not hers, was not legally her son, until the finalisation next July, and that he could be taken away from her. She had looked at the social worker with a new wariness. She was Greg's *mother*, no matter what it was that she didn't know about him.

And there *was* something. Something so complex, so hidden, so powerful about him that she doubted she would ever understand. It frightened her. It drew her to him.

'No,' she had repeated, more calmly.

Melinda had sat back in her chair. 'Good. Then we can work on it together.'

Breanne heard her own reading voice come back into focus and wondered if she'd been skipping sentences or misreading words. The children were about to fly away on the wondrous back of Aslan. Hearing herself speak the magic words – still as if from some distance – she felt herself infected by that magic, the yearning for some all-powerful force of goodness and wisdom that would take away all the pain and heal all the wounds. She paused to take a drink of water and peered over the edge of the book at her father and her son. At that moment, in the firelight, they really were a family. Breanne hoped that these two difficult and beloved people could feel the magic, too.

The fire glowed not two feet from his hand, warming his fingers. His mother's voice was soft, and she was reading to him about a place where animals talked and trees danced and when you thought everything had gone to hell a big lion showed up to take care of things. Greg was drowsy but in no real danger of falling asleep. He realised he was happy, and with the naming of the word felt no panic, no fury, not even surprise. Only more happiness.

' "My children," said Aslan, fixing his eyes on both of them, "you are to be the next King and Queen of Narnia." '

They had just finished decorating the tree, he and Breanne and Andy. The empty place he'd been so worried about on one side was, he had to admit, almost covered with fat blue tinsel rope, and the ornament he'd picked out – a red-cheeked Santa with eyes that rolled when you pulled the tail of his cap – had a place of honor near the top. Breanne said he could pick out one thing for the tree every year, and he'd counted it up. By the time he was eighteen there would be six of his ornaments on the tree. Not very many among all the others, but he'd started late and it was the best he could do.

The yellow cat lay warm beside him. When Greg first came he'd been sure the cat would never like him, and that had made him mad. Now the cat followed him around, jumped into his lap whenever he sat down, slept on his bed at night. Sometimes Greg played too rough – he *knew* he was playing too rough – and then Breanne wouldn't let him play with the cat for a day or two. But he never got badly scratched, and the cat always came back.

Sometimes, once or twice, Greg had been mean on purpose. Shut the cat in the closet, pulled his tail hard, just to see how far he could go before the dumb cat didn't like him anymore. The cat still liked him. He curled up and stretched out along Greg's stomach, soaking up the warmth from Greg's fire, purring, kneading the quilt with his claws. Greg watched through half-closed eyes the cat's yellow-and-white toes flex against the bright patches of the quilt.

He shifted position and tucked the quilt around his knees. Silently he began to play a dangerous little game. He allowed himself to remember, one by one, the times when strange things had happened to him, because of him, the times that had finally convinced him of his power.

It was like walking on a very high wall. It was like diving into dark, cold water. It was like passing your hand back and forth through flames to see how close you could come to getting burned. Breanne's voice in the background made a safe place for Greg to come back to. Recklessly he let the memories form in his mind again.

The handle snapping on the milk pail and the look of shock on Randy's face. The cut opening up on the back of the man's hand. All the toys that had gotten broken over the years, the dolls and bears and trucks. Sherry just learning to walk and he'd made her fall with a little push of his mind, then felt in total amazement the tiny sharp pain of her baby mind pushing back. The litter on the floor of his room that he did not sweep up. The clouds pulling away from the eclipsing moon.

One by one he thought about these things, and nothing happened. Breanne kept reading, reading. The old man Andy sat across the narrow room saying nothing. Nothing happened. Greg kept his breathing normal and his eyes closed. He could feel Breanne's leg against the back of his neck. He could feel the quilt snug around his thighs, and the yellow cat purring against the small of his back.

He had played this game a few times before, when he'd felt loved and safe, and always before the mere thought of his power, the mere memory of it, threatened to bring it back. Then the game itself would become furious and something else would end up broken, somebody else hurt. He had, in fact, been neither safe nor loved.

Now, for the first time, nothing happened, and Greg found himself thinking a grownup word: Coincidence. The handle had been rusty. The bike had been old. Sherry had fallen because she was a little kid, and he had imagined the rest. The clouds had been blown, like any other clouds, away from the face of the moon.

It was crazy to think he had power. Stuff like that didn't happen outside movies and books. He was an ordinary kid with a home and a mother and a bike with a flat tire – just like everybody else.

Feeling both abandoned and cleansed, Greg snuggled against Breanne's leg and opened his eyes a little. A face was staring at him from the flames. He stared. An evil little face, like the face of a bat, like the face of the devil one of his foster mothers had insisted he believe in, a grinning face like his own face and Sherry's with hot brown eyes. It was laughing at him, reaching out with its eyes to claim him again.

Greg sat up and rubbed his eyes and forced himself to cough loud and violently. Breanne gave him some water from her glass and lightly patted his back. When he looked at the fire again it was just a fire and the evil little face wasn't there, but Greg knew from the fury that was leaping inside him where that face had gone.

Andy had always hated Christmas. What he said he hated was the phoniness, the commercialism, the prescribed traditions. What he really hated was his pervasive fear that something about the season would actually touch him, lure him in, and then of course turn out to be false. Andy lived his life on guard, but at Christmas he was even more vigilant than usual; he often had a headache from before Thanksgiving until after New Year's.

This year he had expected things to be even worse. Ruth's silliness, for all he had made fun of her, had shielded him from the worst of it. After thirty-four Christmasses together – many of them, since the girls had left, marked by little more than a white-net Christmas tree on the marble-top table, a package from Claire, a brief and awkward visit from Breanne, the day made different from any other day by only a few small things, and Ruth looking sad – after thirty-four Christmasses like that, Ruth was dead, and Andy hated Christmas.

He had reason for expecting the worst. The boy avoided him, knowing what he knew. Breanne couldn't make *kolachy*; it had taken Ruth, who was not Czech, twenty years to learn to do it right. He'd known Breanne would feel she had to invite him to her house for the holidays and he'd been prepared to refuse, but here he was, it was Christmas Eve, and for some reason his head was barely hurting at all.

He scowled. There was nothing on television worth watching; the commentators seemed to have taken the holidays off, too, as if nothing were going on in the world. If he were home he'd be listening to a tape, one of the books he'd recorded years ago: Barbara Tuchman or Aldous Huxley. His positions had changed over the years. He was no longer a liberal, and now his interest in some of those old books lay in constructing forceful arguments in his mind against all their basic tenets. Ruth had listened to his arguments, though she hadn't understood much. Sometimes, to his annoyance, she had offered an opinion.

Or, at home, he'd be listening to the talk radio station, which didn't go off the air for a 'holiday.' If the subject wasn't something banal like sports or astrology or favorite Christmas traditions, he'd be preparing to make his call, the one call per night he permitted himself.

But he wasn't home, and neither was Ruth. The fact of her absence struck him in the back of the neck. He didn't miss her very often, having decided in advance that it was a waste of time.

Despite himself, despite the headache now lurking behind his eyes, Andy stared at the Christmas tree lights – and found himself pleased. Uncomfortably, he shifted position in the chair. The cat came and curled up peremptorily on his lap. He saw that it was snowing outside, soft zigzags against the pane. The boy's round, secretive face was lit by the firelight. Suddenly Andy felt a sharp, displaced affection for the boy, much like his feelings for Claire and Breanne when they were that age. It had been so much easier when they were small.

Such an emotion was an assault, a violation, and it angered him. His headache leaped forward, seemed almost to leave his head and fill the space between him and the boy before he could bring it back inside.

Breanne was reading a bedtime story. Andy had stayed in the room because he didn't know where else to go in her house, and because he did approve of reading. He did not approve of the drivel she read; he had never allowed his children to read anything escapist. Andy was a realist. He kept himself informed.

He didn't listen to what she was reading after the first few ridiculous words. But he was lulled by the sound of her voice, by the uncharacteristically peaceful look on the face of the boy. It confused him. He watched the fire, feeling almost peaceful himself, though the thoughts of Ruth and of Christmas and of the snake of a headache were curling in the back of his mind.

Andy saw the boy move, to nestle against Breanne. He saw the boy squint into the fire. He saw the pale, hot edge of danger, like firelight on the boy's profile, and he stirred uneasily, making the cat knead its claws in protest. He saw the boy sit bolt upright and cough. He saw Breanne's motherly concern. He knew what had happened. He knew what the boy had seen in the flames, for he had seen it himself a thousand times.

Impassively he turned his own gaze to the fire, and what he saw there was as familiar as his own face, a reminder of the constant danger within which he lived his own life. It was a visage – at one instant a faintly sinister bird like something out of Poe, then a rodent with hooded eyes, then a creature without a name. At the boy's age, or younger, Andy had been terrified and infuriated by the things he and nobody else saw in fire, felt in flesh, smelled in the very air. By now he had learned how to keep them at bay.

The coals subsided and the visage faded away. Andy moved his head too fast and the pain came back like a gunshot. When he looked again there were no images anywhere. The boy had stopped coughing and was lying back on the floor with his eyes closed again – looking,

Andy thought, not peaceful, not comfortable, but calm. That was good. Calmness was the best you could hope for. Andy nodded slightly in approval. Breanne was reading again, and despite himself Andy heard the words: "'In Narnia the beasts lived in great peace and joy and neither the witch nor any other enemy came to trouble that pleasant land for many hundred years.'"

When the telephone rang Andy started, and the cat clawed his thighs and jumped down.

In the kitchen Breanne was trying the *kolachy* again. The filling hadn't been thick enough in the first batch and had seeped out of the pastry onto the cookie sheets, where it glazed and burned. The last tray, though, looked and smelled and tasted (hiding in the corner of the kitchen out of the line of sight of her family in the living room) much as she remembered her mother's. Sadly, she wished she'd paid more attention.

She loved the smell of the sweet rolls baking. She loved Christmas tree lights in a darkened room. Though she didn't in the least *believe*, she loved Christmas carols and candlelight services and the story of the Nativity. She started Christmas shopping in the middle of the summer.

Sliding another pan of the fragrant pastry into the oven, she was vaguely aware of feeling sick again as the aroma drifted up to her. She straightened too quickly and for a few seconds was dizzy. Lately she'd been having episodes of vertigo and nausea, and it worried her that she might be coming down with something. She didn't want to be sick for Christmas.

From the living room she thought she heard her son say something to her father and her father reply. She didn't catch the words, and so could remind herself that their relationship was none of her business. All she caught was the sound of it – a warm and friendly murmur, like a family, like Christmas.

Breanne hadn't dared feel safe and peaceful since the terrible fight with Greg. Even now, just remembering it, she was conscious of a preparatory rush of adrenaline that made her tremble and breathe hard. She had never been so furious with anyone in her life – not even with her father had she come so close to losing control.

'Anger,' Melinda had said, nodding, 'is a pretty powerful thing. Sometimes it actually seems to have a life of its own.'

Breanne ran the sink full of hot, soapy water and lowered into it a stack of baking dishes. The timer buzzed and she was just taking out the last, and perfect, batch of *kolachy* when the telephone rang.

'Breanne. This is Melinda.'

It's Christmas Eve. She's calling on Christmas Eve. Something terrible has happened. 'Yes, Melinda.'

'I just got a call from Sherry's worker. Breanne, Sherry's dead.'

The certain knowledge that her son was in great danger came to Breanne full force before she could place who Sherry was, and she turned to look at him where he lay before the fire. Then she knew, and closed her eyes, and saw with astonishment the dead face of a child she'd never seen in life. Sherry. Greg's little sister, of whom he almost never spoke. Sherry, who had stayed with her mother, who hadn't been taken away.

She carried the phone into the kitchen before she asked, 'What happened?'

'There was a fire in the apartment.'

'She was left alone?' Breanne said flatly.

'No, her mother's boyfriend was there. He's okay. Smoke inhalation. He tried to go in after her.'

'Greg,' said Breanne softly, glancing again into the living room, where, in the dim and multicolored light from the Christmas tree and the fire, neither her father nor her son seemed to have been disturbed by the ringing of the phone on Christmas Eve. 'Oh, Greg.'

'I know,' said the social worker. In the background Breanne could hear voices, which abruptly quieted as if Melinda had hushed them with a gesture. 'Do you need help telling him?'

'Not tonight. It's Christmas Eve. Our first Christmas together.'

'I could come over on Saturday.'

'No. Thanks. He's my son.'

There was a pause. Then Melinda said, 'I'm sorry, Breanne. I'm so sorry. Call me if you need to.' Breanne nodded, thanked her, hung up. She stood alone in the kitchen for awhile, aware of a slight sickness in the pit of her stomach and of the steady pounding of her heart. Then she stacked some warm *kolachy* onto a tray decorated with glittering poinsettias, arranged a fan of red napkins across one end, and went to spend Christmas Eve with her family.

10

He could see her.

It was Saturday morning. Breanne woke up again and rolled over to check the clock. Almost nine thirty. She listened for sounds from downstairs and faintly heard screeches and chuckles from *Popeye* and *Roadrunner* and *The Flintstones* and others whose names she wouldn't recognise. Life as a mother had been much easier since she'd decided that Saturday morning cartoons wouldn't turn Greg's mind into a vast wasteland.

She raised her head to readjust the pillow, and the effort exhausted her. Her limbs ached. Her mind dipped and bobbed like a kite cut loose from its string. Dimly she was aware of snow-softened noises outside her window: cars going by, the cries of children – not Greg – playing. She went back to sleep.

He could see her. Small. Always smaller than he was. Blond hair, the color his had been before it darkened. Before she was born. He was sent to his first foster home because Mommy couldn't take care of him, too. 'You understand, don't you, Greg? Mommy loves you.' Later he went home, but never for very long. Sherry was always at home.

He could see her. Her eyes were on him like hard brown bugs. She followed him everywhere he went. She got in his way. Now she was dead. Breanne had told him – holding him, making him look at her – that Sherry was dead.

Breanne stirred under the covers. Her body didn't seem to be her own. Her fingers seemed excruciatingly far away. With a conscious effort she brought them to her face and wonderingly touched her lips, her ears. She felt as if she were under water, held in a giant flotation tank whose boundaries she could not reach and whose lid she could not hope to lift. It frightened her, but even the fear was sluggish and out of reach. She tried to sit up, and felt sick and dizzy and all at once so sad that she burst into tears. Something was wrong. Something was wrong with her. Something was wrong with Greg. Suffused with a sense of tragedy, of impossible responsibility, and of overwhelming fatigue, Breanne – still crying – went back to sleep.

'Greg, get her out of here!'

He could see her, giggling and shrieking as he pulled her out of the room. Above and behind them, the voices and the noise, the sound of blows, the heavy breathing. He could see her. She was his little sister, always smaller than he was, growing in their mother's belly, where he couldn't get back in, sitting on their mother's lap when he was too big to do that anymore, sucking at their mother's breast when he couldn't even watch because he was a big boy now, following him around, getting in his way, never getting hit like he did because she was smaller and a girl and he took care of her.

She watched what he did, and she learned. She could do the weird stuff, too. But he could never get her to use it on people who were bad. She used it on him. He'd hear a crash and he'd run into his room and his model plane would be in pieces on the floor, and Sherry would be sitting on his bed with her hands in her lap grinning at him. They'd be on their way to school and he'd look down and his zipper would be split, and Sherry wasn't even anywhere around. He could never tell on her, either. Nobody would believe him, and if they did, then they'd know about his power, too. She could do it better than him, but she wouldn't do it right.

He could see her. He knew what had happened. She didn't do it right this time, either. If he had been there he could have done it for her, but now she was dead.

Breanne had been feeling like this for weeks. At first she'd thought she had the flu. She'd taken a sick day and slept until Greg got home from school, but it hadn't helped. The fatigue was like nothing she'd ever experienced before. The nausea waxed and waned, sometimes just a dull discomfort in the pit of her stomach, sometimes an assault that doubled her over the basin. Intense, rootless depression alternated madly with elation, and none of it seemed to belong to her.

She struggled out of sleep, certain there was something she had to do. But once she was awake her mind refused to bring whatever it was to the surface. She forced herself to think systematically about Greg, about the work she'd brought home from the office, about scrubbing the kitchen floor, but the specific thoughts melted away as soon as she thought them, leaving only a free-floating residue of worry.

She hid her face in the pillow and, as if dark water were covering her again, fell asleep.

He could see her. She wouldn't leave him alone. Her face, her whining little voice, her mean little hands – always doing something to him, always herself in danger. She followed him everywhere. It drove him crazy. Momma had given him up and not Sherry, because Momma thought Sherry was the good kid. Now she was dead.

He knew what had happened. The man had been hurting her, and so she had exploded the apartment. He wouldn't have been able to do that. Sherry had done it, though, and the man had gotten out anyway, and she was dead, and she still wouldn't leave him alone.

He pushed at her face in his mind. It fell to pieces and then put itself together again. He tore at it and watched her bleed, but no matter what he did she was still there.

He sat up in bed, turned on the lamp, and then with both hands threw the lamp against the wall.

The crash brought Breanne out of bed before she was quite conscious. The fatigue still pressed on her shoulders and head, the nausea still gripped her abdomen, but she pulled on her robe and pushed her feet into her slippers and hurried downstairs, holding tightly to the rail.

As she opened the door to Greg's room she suddenly knew what was wrong with her, and the realisation brought a shocking ice-cold instant of clarity to her mind. She was pregnant. She was going to have a baby.

She switched on the ceiling light and rapidly took in the scene. Greg was sitting up in bed, his back to the wall, screaming. She had time to notice that there were no tears. She had time to see the broken pieces of the lamp in the corner, the frayed cord still plugged into the wall. She had time for a moment of irritation, because she had given the lamp back to him only yesterday after he'd promised to take care of it. Greg threw something at her as she entered the room; she didn't see his hand move, but something thumped against the wall over her head.

'Greg!' she shouted, and bent to unplug the cord, careful in her haste not to touch the exposed wires. 'Greg, stop it!'

But he wasn't going to stop it, she could see. It was as if something had taken possession of him, and when she touched him she could feel its power. Sharp awareness of the change inside her own body meshed with new understanding of the change that took place inside her son when he was like this. Adrenaline pumped through her as she was seized by a definitive urge to protect – to protect herself, to protect Greg, to protect the baby, to protect them all from the awful thing that was raging now inside this room.

She flung herself onto the bed and threw her arms around Greg. He thrust her away. She didn't see his arms move but she was on the floor, panting, reaching for him, and she grabbed his hair because it was the only thing she could reach. He kicked at her, but his feet were tangled in the bedclothes. She fought to her knees, and, still holding his hair in one hand, managed to wrap the blankets more tightly around him so that he couldn't move very much. Even so, she felt a pain in her stomach and her head as though he had struck her, and she caught her breath with a sound like a sob.

'Greg!'

He rolled onto the floor and she maneuvered herself so that she was sitting on him, straddling his chest, pinning his arms with her knees. With her hands she held his head, as gently as she could amid all that fury. He was still screaming, and she saw with relief that now there were tears streaming down his cheeks, making him cough and seeming to diffuse some of the rage.

'Greg,' she told him, in a firm voice which maybe now he could hear. 'I won't let you hurt yourself. I won't let you hurt me.'

She hoped it was true. She hoped she could do that. Again she felt the stab of pain inside her body, and she thought of the baby whose presence she had discovered only a few long minutes ago, but the pain went away and she watched Greg's face. He struggled under her, but wrapped in the blankets he was like a baby, swaddled against the dangerous forces in the world, protected against himself. He arched his back under her and tried to twist out of her grasp. She was aware of her nightgown pulling up over her knees and her robe coming open in front, but she held on, making crooning noises in her throat which probably he didn't hear but which served to soothe her, to let her concentrate. When he opened his eyes to stare at her the light from the ceiling lamp glistened in them.

'I'm so scared!' he croaked.

'I know.'

'I'm so scared!'

'And you're sad about Sherry,' she tried. 'Sherry's dead.'

He nodded, and then he broke into tears – real tears, childish tears. The kind of grieving that allowed her to move to his side and take him in her arms. He cried and cried, and when the nausea and fatigue came over her again she accepted them with a kind of awe.

11

He could have told her he wanted to go downtown, but that would have spoiled the fun. He would be in big trouble when he got home – probably grounded again, and that was a drag – but it was worth it. He loved downtown. Loved the bright concrete, the thin trees in buckets along the new mall, the people with their arms full of packages or their hands in their pockets, hurrying through the cold air and, he thought, wishing for snow.

He bought a hot dog off a cart with a red-and-white-striped awning. The guy who sold it to him was wearing dirty red-and-white-striped mittens, and Greg thought that was funny. A guy in a green ski mask was dealing dope out of the alley between Woolworth's and Thom McAn's. Greg shook his head at him and said knowledgeably, 'No way, man.'

He stepped aboard the sleek shuttle bus cruising the mall and wedged himself among all the people to grab a seat, keeping his eyes away from the fat old lady with all the packages who clung to the pole in front of him. She scowled at him and clicked her teeth. Gleefully he pushed at her with his mind, and the bus stopped at the next stop, and two of her boxes fell. Greg leaned over to pick them up, not bothering to hide his grin. She snatched them out of his hand and waddled off the bus without thanking him, almost getting caught in the doors. Greg stuck his tongue out at her swaying back, but didn't give up his seat in order to watch her walk down the street.

He got off the bus at Tremont and watched the ice skaters on Zeckendorff Plaza for awhile. He thought about them falling and they fell, one by one by one, except for one pretty lady in a baby-blue parka and a white muff who smiled at him every time she went around the rink and didn't fall once, though he thought insistently about her falling on her ass.

He walked through May D&F because he hated it. It was all glass and polished chrome and thick carpets so you couldn't hear your footsteps, and he was always slightly disoriented there. He couldn't imagine how anyone could actually shop in that store, and anyway the prices were high. Breanne had bought him a shirt here once, and it was scratchy. The sales clerks ignored him, as if he couldn't possibly want to *buy* anything, or watched him like hawks, as if he was going to rip them off. He thought about it, the bastards. Instead, he kept his hands in his pockets and thought about all the glass things falling off onto the bouncy red carpet, and some of them did.

Downtown ground and coughed with the constant noise of heavy equipment. Greg stopped to watch a crane lift something to the top of a building. He stared so long at the bright-orange crane and the black building ribs and the blue sky and the silver reflections off the other buildings nearby that everything seemed to be falling down on him and he staggered and had to look away. When he looked back, the cherry-picker had opened its jaws like a dinosaur, deposited something on the high scaffold, and started down again. Greg frowned and concentrated. He heard someone yell, and a piece of metal floated from the scaffold to the street, landing with a high-pitched crash in the hard-hat area. Laughing, Greg walked away.

He opened the front door of Woolworth's and frowned at the heavy smell of sweat and dust and fried chicken. There were always so many people in Woolworth's. Screaming kids, and cool black girls popping gum and strolling in threes and fours down the narrow aisles so nobody else could get past, and smart-ass white dudes pushing you out of the way with their boots and their greasy voices, and old ladies with ripping paper sacks in both hands picking their way along as if they were walking in a minefield. Greg hated Woolworth's. He walked through it every time he came downtown, just to see if he could stand it.

He rode the escalator to the basement, where half a dozen middle-aged ladies fingered dirty cloth in the fabric department. He walked through the stereo department and made a couple of tapes slide to the floor. His fists were in his pockets. His hat was pulled low over his ears. He rode the other escalator up to the main floor again, and glared at the back of the hot-shit dude who had pushed his way in front of him, and as he was getting off the escalator the dude tripped and almost fell.

The temperature seemed to be going up a little. Store awnings were dripping onto the sidewalk. A big piece of ice fell off a building into the alley. A very short man in a black coat that almost touched the snow and a black hat that almost touched his collar was walking back and forth at the bus stop on Curtis Street, shouting about the end of the world. Nobody was paying any attention to him; people were chatting with each other, or frowning distractedly as they waited for the bus, or scuffing at the melting ice. It made Greg laugh to think that this guy might really know something about the end of the world and nobody was paying any attention to him.

Two girls walked by, one of them carrying a radio the size of a suitcase. The Beastie Boys blared out onto the snowy sidewalk. The girls glanced at Greg. They were a lot older than he was, probably sixteen or seventeen, and one of them winked at him in a way that made him mad. 'Hey,' he said to her. 'Got a cigarette?'

'Are you kidding?' The girls laughed shrilly, and the Beastie Boys quit singing with a rush of loud music and the DJ's fast voice.

'Hey,' Greg said again, following them. 'You got a cigarette?'

'Get lost, kid,' said the girl with the radio.

'Fuck you,' Greg told them flatly, and followed them

67

awhile longer, staring at their wet white sneakers, until the one with the radio slipped and the radio fell out of her hand to slide along the sidewalk and tip over in a pile of slush. Satisfied, Greg put his cold hands into his pockets and turned away.

He walked through a wooden tunnel where a sidewalk had been torn up for construction. The walls were covered with graffiti, most of which made little sense to him. El Salvador. Landlords. Names and dates he didn't recognise. If he'd had a magic marker or a can of spray paint maybe he would have written something, too, though he didn't know what. At the middle of the tunnel, where it bent outward into the street like an elbow, someone had set up a table that made it almost impossible to get through. On the table were pamphlets and pieces of paper, and tacked to the wooden wall was a poster proclaiming 'Harry McAllister for President.' A man with a gray face and a lopsided moustache stood beside the table, and when he saw Greg pause he spoke directly to him: 'How would you like to work in Washington, DC, my boy?'

Startled, Greg said, 'Sure.'

'Here.' Harry McAllister came out from the table and blocked Greg's way, so that nobody else could get through the tunnel, either. This formed a little crowd, an audience, and Harry McAllister raised his voice. 'I represent the Peace and Prosperity Party. I represent all that is good and right about America. Do you believe in all that is good and right about America, my boy?'

'Sure,' said Greg again, grinning.

'Of course you do. We all do. And I will be the next President of the United States. And when I am in Washington, my boy, I will remember you for my cabinet. We need fresh blood. Young ideas. A contribution would be most appreciated, my boy, to help in our glorious work.'

'I ain't got no money,' Greg said.

'Well, well, that's all right. Here, take some of these.' He loaded Greg's arms with pamphlets, all with tricolored pictures of the American flag and the face of Harry McAllister looking off as if into the future.

Greg carried the pamphlets to the other end of the tunnel and then let them blow away into the slush. Behind him the people who had been prevented from walking through the tunnel were coming out now, some of them acting as if Harry McAllister had not existed, others looking irritated or amused or embarrassed. Nobody seemed to be taking him seriously.

Greg heard a man in a fancy topcoat say to his high-heeled female companion, 'Poor man. He needs help. Somebody should come and take him away.' Greg stared at the couple as they walked by. The woman saw him staring and frowned disapprovingly. They walked by too quickly for him to be able to do anything, though he would have loved to see them fall on their fancy asses in the dirty snow.

He made a snowball and tossed it under the wheels of a bus, liking the way it crushed. He bought a flower from a girl on the corner and stuck it into the zipper of his parka. He watched the mechanical joggers in the window of the sporting-goods store. He listened to the bells from the carillon in the top of the D&F Tower. He stood in the weird reflections of the 17th Street canyon and listened to the way the city noises echoed and spun.

When he stood for a long time in an alley and concentrated on the gray pile of slush that had been shoveled against the building, a hole appeared in it. When he watched the girl with the flowers, who had been snotty to him, her cart tipped and all the wrong-colored carnations scattered on the sidewalk around her. When he crossed the street against the light and a car didn't stop for him, slowed down and turned the corner anyway and actually brushed against him, he concentrated on it as it made its way down the street; it pulled at an angle over to the curb, as if maybe one of its tires had suddenly gone flat.

Having played, having practiced as much as he needed to that day, being cold and hungry by now and a little worried about what Breanne would say, Greg caught the next bus home.

12

'Limits,' said the social worker – talking, Greg thought, just like a social worker. Her level gaze took in both him and his mother. He didn't look at either one of them very long. 'Anger is okay. Anger is healthy. But it's not okay to hurt yourself or somebody else. There have to be limits.'

Greg stared at his shoes, trying to imagine himself somewhere else. His shoes were wearing through on the sides already because his feet were so wide. He'd spent all his January clothing allowance, and Breanne had warned him at the time to save some for shoes later on, but maybe, if he worked it right, she'd buy him another pair anyway. His feet were growing faster than the rest of him. Mr Franconi said maybe he was like a puppy; you would tell how big he was going to be by the size of his feet.

The trick on himself worked. Thinking about something else, he wasn't in danger of cracking the social worker's head open or blowing up her office. He tried, in fact, to move the frog-shaped ashtray on her desk, but nothing happened.

Greg hated social workers. They didn't keep their promises. They didn't speak plain English. They messed around with stuff they didn't understand. 'Anger,' she said, like she knew what she was talking about. 'Limits.' He twisted in his chair to express his extreme contempt and avoided bringing his mother into his line of vision at all. Lately she'd been quiet and sick a lot, spending a lot of time in her room, and he knew it was because of him.

When Mr Franconi saw Greg getting mad in school, he'd say to him – quietly if they were at their desks close together in the front of the room, or shouting at him across the playground – 'Greg. Get yourself together.' And he did. The first time he'd surprised himself. He'd been about to deck that hot shit from the other sixth-grade class, and when he'd heard Mr Franconi say that, something had happened inside his head, and all he'd done was spit on the ground and walk away. He'd felt good about it, too. 'It'll be all right, Greg. Greg. Get yourself together.'

'Greg,' said the social worker sharply. 'Listen to me. You *can* learn to control it. It is *not* stronger than you are.'

Fuck you, he told her in his mind, but with less savagery than he wanted to be feeling. Fuck you, bitch, you just stay the hell away from me. Do you know who you're talking to here? Do you know how close you are to really getting hurt? Trying to muster a little fury, he concentrated on the single cigarette butt in the cheek of the frog. But when it was broken he couldn't be sure it had been in one piece in the first place. For one awful moment he thought he was going to cry.

'Greg,' said the social worker. He saw, horrified, that she was coming over to him, kneeling, trying to take his hands. He almost punched her in the nose. He wouldn't have meant to. He wouldn't have dared to. Melinda put her hands on his knees. 'Greg. Listen. You are not responsible for Sherry's death.'

He gasped. He said against his will, 'I wasn't with her.'

'You couldn't have saved her even if you had been. You probably would have been killed, too.'

'What did she look like?' he asked, almost in a whisper. 'After.'

The social worker nodded. 'She was on the floor near the door. She was badly burned.' He held his breath, waiting for more. 'When you're burned like that, your skin turns red and kind of – blackened.'

He suspected she was making this up. Sherry had died in Chicago. The social worker hadn't even been there. It didn't matter. He wanted to believe her. He needed a picture. Something he could take apart and put back together in his mind. 'Was there blood?'

'Yes.' He nodded. Slowly he let out his breath. Melinda was watching him. 'The whole place just blew up,' she said. 'They still don't know what caused it.'

I know, he thought. He was very tired. He leaned his head back against the hard chair. He felt the social worker's fingers around his knees, as if she were holding him down. His mother wasn't touching him; maybe she didn't love him, or maybe she wasn't in the room. Not looking at her, he couldn't even be sure she existed. He summoned up Sherry's face – first the way he remembered it, then the way it must have looked when she died. When he tried to make the face fall apart, it didn't; it just faded slowly away until he could barely see it anymore.

Anger. Breanne listened to the social worker talking to Greg, and her own anger was a sweet burst inside her, sweet and rich and satisfying. Addicting, she thought. *Anger.* She was tired of living with everyone else's anger – her father's, her son's, her sister Claire's that had driven her away. It was time to claim some anger of her own.

Anger. She forced herself to look at their faces: Melinda's face, earnest and sharp and curtained behind her hair; Greg's petulant and secretive as always. She wanted to shake them, both of them. They both thought they knew what they were doing. She wanted to put herself between them. She wanted to get up and leave the room, stride down the brown hallway to the elevator, punch the 'Down' button, plummet to the ground floor in the tiny padded cage that would echo with her shouting, walk through the crowds of pale young mothers with their harried youngsters waiting in line before the one calm eligibility tech for food stamps, through the two sets of double glass doors, past the black-uniformed and silver-badged security guard who gulped coffee and didn't acknowledge questions – and *out*. Leave them. Leave them to each other, this impossible child with this arrogant social worker. Leave her father to make his own angry peace with the world that was surely falling apart, though not fast enough to suit him. *Leave*.

There was not even space in the narrow interview room for her to cross her legs without kicking Greg. Melinda did not even have her own office, only a desk in a huge partitioned room. Breanne reflected on the fact that in her own office – in a company that handled penny stock investments for the would-be *nouveaux riches* and frightened new poor of Denver's erratic oil boom-and-bust economy – there were more than enough rooms, with more than enough space in them, and windows, and soft leather swivel chairs around polished hexagonal tables, and a good coffee pot always full. Here, certainly, the idea was not to impress the customers, who, though called clients, were no less the agency's livelihood, and who were already impressed by their own need and by the system's power to meet or deny it. Breanne had felt that herself. Here the rooms were cramped, windowless, hot; there were never enough to go around, so interviews had to be scheduled well in advance and even then there were conflicts sometimes, a wild-eyed family waiting in the lobby to talk about their incest while a welfare mother painstakingly signed her work contract at the table with the cracked veneer. The weak coffee cost fifty cents in the basement cafeteria.

Anger. It startled her that this much anger should give her this much pleasure. She'd always thought of anger as poison, needing to be purged. She'd never thought of it as something that belonged to her. Irritation, maybe, when Greg broke something again; frustration when a customer's account got screwed up; impatience, she remembered, when her father told her mother to get him another cup of coffee and her mother did. But never anger. Never fury. It seemed to Breanne that she had never been angry before in her life, and she rather liked it.

She hadn't told anyone she was pregnant. She hadn't written to Jeff, although she owed him an answer anyway to his last friendly-as-usual letter. She hadn't even been to the doctor. But lately, in addition to the nausea and fatigue encumbering her like a wet wool blanket, her breasts were so tender that rolling onto her stomach at night would wake her up with the pain. She was sure. And she was furious.

Suddenly she could not bear another second in the closed room with these two people who, sooner or later, would want something from her. She got to her feet, interrupting them. 'I'm going to the bathroom,' she announced, and left the room, fantasising that she didn't have to come back.

With Breanne gone the room felt different. Greg stirred uncomfortably in his chair and tried to put his feet up, but they wouldn't fit between the rungs. He was tired and hot. He wanted to be anywhere but here. Vaguely he wished something would break in here, but he couldn't concentrate enough to make it happen and he knew it wouldn't happen without him.

'Tell me something, Greg.' Looking right at him, Melinda broke a pencil in two. He jumped as if the snap had been an explosion, and stared at her. She smiled. 'What's it like when you're mad?'

'I don't know.'

'Bullshit.'

It surprised him that a social worker would talk like that and he waited for her to say something else, but she didn't so he didn't either.

After a moment she said, 'If you don't want to answer a question you can say, "I don't want to answer that," but I won't buy "I don't know." Not from you.'

She stopped talking again. He just waited. He was tired, and dully angry, but he was also excited. This was the kind of game that all grownups, and especially social workers, played that he thought was stupid and terribly important at the same time. An important play was about to be made, a play so big that he'd remember it all his life like an instant replay. He had no idea what his move was supposed to be. He waited for a signal.

'So, Greg,' Melinda said, leaning back in her chair with the two halves of the pencil jagged and bright yellow in her hands. 'What's it like? A fire? A storm? A raging animal? What?'

He was astonished, violated. She knew all the images. He thought about saying he didn't want to answer the question, but he did want to. 'An eclipse,' he said to confuse her, curling his lip. She didn't say anything, just raised her eyebrows and waited. He took a deep breath. 'It's like I'm holding a gun. I just have to point it, and somebody gets hurt, or something gets broken, or the eclipse happens.' Under his breath he added softly, like a much younger boy, 'Bang.'

'Except,' Melinda said, 'that you get hurt, too. It's like the gun explodes in your hand.'

Not exactly, he thought, but close enough. He nodded once.

The social worker was silent for awhile and he almost forgot where he was, almost stopped wondering where Breanne had gone – almost, in fact, fell asleep. But a small hot part of his mind, like a laser, stayed awake.

Finally Melinda spoke and her voice was different, so he opened his eyes to look at her. 'Let me tell you something, Greg. You're so big on images and metaphors, let me give you another one. When you start getting mad and you know something bad is going to happen if you don't stop, imagine you're on a bicycle. You're carrying an explosive in your basket.'

'Nitroglycerine,' he said at once, thinking of some movie, or TV show or something.

'Nitroglycerine. If you take a corner too fast, you could blow yourself and everything else to smithereens. So when you want to turn a corner, what do you do? Do you turn the wheel real sharply?' She gestured with her hands and tilted her body in her chair.

'No.'

'No. All you have to do when you're on this dangerous bicycle is *think* about turning. *Think* about getting out of danger. *Think* about avoiding things you might run into.

That's all. *Think* about it, and the bike responds without your ever turning the handlebars.'

He knew what she was talking about. When he'd first learned to ride a bike – late, when he was nine, on a rusted red bike that everybody else used, too – he'd always been running into things, skidding out on corners, crashing over curbs. He'd finally figured out that he was trying too hard. All you had to do was *think* about it, and it came naturally.

'Nitroglycerine, huh?' The thought pleased him.

'Nitroglycerine.'

He nodded. He wondered where Breanne was, and knew he'd find her somewhere in the building. The social worker stood up and held out her hand. He took it, awkwardly, looked at her, and asked, ' Are you sure she's dead?'

'Yes, Greg.' She looked at him gently, but to his surprise she didn't hug him. He hated social workers who hugged you like it was part of their job. She even let him pull his hand away. 'Yes. I'm sure.'

13

Making love with Jeff had been as awkward as any first time, hardly leavened at all by the fact that they'd known each other for years. When they'd kissed, his lips had barely moved. Surprised and embarrassed, thinking she'd made a mistake, Breanne had stepped back and all but wiped her mouth on her sleeve. But he'd caught her shoulders and drawn her to him again.

After a while she'd gently pulled free and whispered, 'Wait. My diaphragm,' trying to make it sound like part of the foreplay although she was clumsily fumbling in her purse.

'You won't need it,' he'd said out loud. 'I've had a vasectomy.'

She was dressed in a fraction of the time it took them to run the pregnancy test, but sitting on the tall examination table she still felt exposed. The doctor – a high-cheek-boned ice-blond named Ilse Daniels with equally icy hands – came back into the room, shut the door, and regarded her calmly. 'Yes. The test is positive. You are pregnant.'

Breanne's head swam.

After an evening of animated conversation, they'd hardly talked at all in bed. Neither of them knew what the other liked, or how to ask or tell. When he'd whispered, 'That was *nice*,' she'd climaxed, arching high in the dark above him, hands braced back on his thighs. She never felt him come. After a while he'd just stopped moving, and it had seemed graceless to inquire.

'My God,' she breathed now.

'I'd say you are about nine weeks along.'

They had lain still for a time, and Breanne had nearly fallen asleep. Then his hand had slid gently between her legs. It was sweet and easier the second time, and she had felt him come inside her, and he had sighed.

'Is it possible,' Breanne asked the doctor carefully, 'for a man who has had a vasectomy to impregnate someone?'

Dr Daniels snapped the chart shut and leaned back against the desk. 'Quite possible. And more common than we would like to think. One in a thousand cases, perhaps. It is as though the sealing of the tubes can sometimes actually stimulate the tissue to form a new channel, through which the sperm can then travel to their hearts' content.' Cooly, she smiled.

Late that afternoon as she sat in the quiet house trying to read, Breanne kept thinking: luck. Coincidence. Odds of one thousand to one. Nearly all the important events in her life seemed to have happened that way. She seldom had a sense of deciding, of making things happen, but rather of staying ready. She'd been ready for Greg. Maybe she had been ready for this pregnancy. Maybe in another seven months she would be ready for this baby.

On her way home from the doctor's office she'd mailed a note to Jeff. She didn't know what she'd do if he wanted some part of this. Certainly she had no desire to marry him. Certainly she didn't want an abortion. At nineteen or twenty she might have considered that, or relinquishing the baby for adoption, but now there was no justification for thinking herself unready for motherhood, and this child was not unwanted.

She ought to be knitting booties, or a yellow-and-white crib blanket. But it took an effort of will, a leap of faith, for her to believe there was a baby. She had no doubt she was *pregnant* – the nausea was with her all the time now, the fatigue had settled over her like a placenta, her breasts hurt to the touch, and, besides, the doctor had said so. But she couldn't imagine a *baby*.

Gladly she heard Greg come home from school. On days

like this, when she was so profoundly out of sorts that the mere thought of complicated portfolios and nervous clients sent her burrowing back under the covers or reaching for an exotic novel, she sometimes resented his three o'clock intrusion. Not today. Today she was ready for him, and she called, 'Hello.'

'Hi.' He came into the room where she was, smelling sweetly of fresh air. 'What are you reading?'

'A novel about a tropical island.'

'That stuff's not real.'

'No, but it's fun. Greg,' she said, 'I'm pregnant.'

'Huh?' Startled, of course. Caught by surprise. She hadn't intended to tell him like that, but these days her mind was so foggy that she could often not quite control how she said things. Now that it was out she could only say it again: 'I'm pregnant. That's why I've been feeling so – weird.'

'Jesus.'

She held out her hand. He took it. His hand was nearly as big as hers, and already a little roughened. 'We're going to have a baby,' she said, though she couldn't believe that herself; she said it to make it real for him.

The next morning she told her father. It was Saturday and she stopped by his house to drop off some gladioli bulbs she'd decided to replace with annuals along her back fence. She handed him the sack, stood with her hands in her pockets just inside the door of his house – in which, after all, she had not grown up – and said, 'Daddy, I have something exciting to tell you.'

She saw his eyes darken and deepen, saw the anger swell, the love rage and surge. She felt her own anger – no match for his, certainly, but gaining.

'I'm pregnant.'

He actually took a step back, and at first she didn't recognise the look on his face. Then she realised that she had pleased him. 'Well,' he said. 'Well.'

'We're going to have a baby,' she said, to make it real for him.

She and Greg had spent a wonderful evening together. She'd brought out a book of color photos of embryos and fetuses in various stages of development and they'd marveled together at the tiny fishlike creatures, the minuscule ears and toes, the faces.

'I never looked like that,' he said, and raised his eyes to hers.

'Sure you did. Inside Debbie's body. Inside her womb. See?' She traced with her fingertips the protective uterine outline, the astonishing length of the umbilical cord. 'That's how you started. Debbie gave you life.' His face glowed when she said that, and she felt as if she'd given him nearly as precious a gift. He finally fell asleep on the couch with the book open on his chest, a bedtime story.

Now it was as if her father remembered his place. His shoulders stiffened. His eyes seemed almost to hood. His face became closed and familiar again. 'A baby,' he said, not looking at her. 'I hope you've thought this through.'

At that moment, saving her from having to reply, Greg came up the driveway from where he'd been investigating motorcycle tracks on the shoulder of the road. 'Can I stay here for awhile?'

Andy said nothing. Breanne glanced at him and then said, trying to keep the curiosity out of her voice, 'It's all right with me if it's all right with your grandpa.'

'I'll be working in the yard all day,' Andy said.

'I'll help.' His eagerness made Breanne wince.

'Okay.' Breanne looked at them both. Her son's face was bright and very young. Her father was scowling and pretending that he didn't want them to notice. 'I'll pick you up later this afternoon.'

It was a bright March day, cool enough to make bare hands hurt after awhile, with the first fuzz of new leaves on the trees. Every spring it seemed to Andy that the huge trees around his house took longer than they should to bud, and he was well into brooding about that – how much it would cost to have them taken out when they died, how unsightly the house would look without them –

before he had to admit that the leaves were in fact coming and the trees were not dead.

He raked and shoveled away the mulch around the roses, scowling because the leaves and grass clippings hadn't completely decomposed. Damn dry air. He'd lived in Colorado nearly nine years now – having left without a pang the house he and Ruth had lived in all their married life and having gone along, against his unspoken better judgment, with Ruth's desire to be near the only one of their daughters whose whereabouts they could be sure of from day to day – but he still wasn't used to the climate. In Pennsylvania you put a seed in the ground and if it didn't rot it grew. In Colorado the things you wanted to rot wouldn't, the flowers all looked spindly and washed-out, and grasshoppers ate the tomato plants.

He saw, though, that the trunks of the rosebushes were beginning to green. Ruth had always picked the first yellow rose for the vase in the middle of the table. Andy could never remember until they bloomed which bush was the yellow, which the salmon, the scarlet, the white. Ruth would have known.

Breanne had brought the gladioli bulbs in a grocery sack, paper instead of plastic. They were probably dried out by now. He reached in and extracted a handful of tubers and tendrils and soil. Cupping it in both hands, he gently pushed at it, feeling suddenly and impossibly as if he were holding a baby. A deformed baby. A dead baby. A baby to whom his hands could impart life.

Children were starving all over the world. Helping one or a dozen or a thousand wouldn't make a dent in the problem. Children were born addicted to heroin. Children killed other children with shotguns and deliberately drowned them in swimming pools. He read about it. The world was in a mess. Not that it affected him personally, but he liked to keep informed.

The mass seemed to move in his hands. Shaken, Andy closed his fists around it and sat back on his heels. His head hurt. His vision blurred. He tore the bulbs apart from each other, bright broken white, gleaming like teeth or

81

bone. A baby. She was going to have a baby.

He knew what it would be safe to feel, and he struggled to feel it. Fear for her and for the child to be brought unwillingly into this world. Moral distaste that she wasn't married. Fury with the nameless father of the child – if she even knew who it was. He worked hard for those feelings and his head throbbed, but what he clearly felt was joy. And the unmistakable, irrational suspicion that, because of this, his life might have been worth something after all.

The raw spring earth was littered with dry sprigs of last year's pinwheel petunias. Andy knelt and with the trowel in one hand dug a four-inch-deep trough, with the other hand clutching to his chest the bundle of bulbs and dirt. The afternoon sun slanted across the back of his head, warming the bald spot which would redden and roughen in the summer sun. Ruth used to kiss his bald spot. He could feel his pulse racing in his wrists. For a moment he even thought he could see it, and then he turned his wrists to the ground.

'That's not deep enough.'

Andy jumped, and was enormously irritated. The boy had been inside watching television since he'd been here, and Andy had practically forgotten him. He dropped a bulb into the trench, covered it with soil, packed it with the heel of his hand, and said without looking up, 'Yes, it is.'

'That one's broken. It won't grow.'

'It's fine.'

'It's too early to plant flowers anyway. Ground's too cold.'

'It doesn't get cold enough here for the ground to freeze most winters. These are spring bulbs. This is when your spring bulbs.'

'Those kind of flowers will look dumb here.'

Andy positioned another bulb in the trench and continued with a careful row of them, eight inches apart, four inches deep, tips up. When the trench was full he still had half a sack of bulbs, and he didn't know where to put them. Stiffly he got to his feet and walked the length of the trench, tamping the dirt with his weight.

'We're going to have a baby,' Greg said from behind him.

Andy thought frantically: The glads might also look all right along the south side of the house, where Ruth had had marigolds. He picked up the sack and walked away.

Greg followed. 'My mom's going to have a baby,' he said.

'She's not your mother,' Andy said before he thought, and then amended, 'Not your real mother.'

'She's as real as they come.' Something in the boy's voice made Andy turn to look at him, and he saw the dark-brown eyes flicker as if they were searching for something in his face – some vulnerability, some way in. It struck Andy that his knowledge of the boy was fragmentary, his warning during the eclipse foolish and without referent. The boy was dangerous in a way that Andy did not understand, and now that he was going to have his own grandchild it was obvious that there was no kinship, no bond. Relieved, he turned away. The pain in his head moved as if it were being guided.

He planted two more long rows of gladioli bulbs along the south wall of the house, and threw the rest away. He wouldn't tell her. The boy had disappeared again and Andy put him out of his mind. He arranged his thoughts around the Social Security system. Any fool could have predicted its imminent bankruptcy. Too many people expecting too much. He didn't see how they'd ever straighten it out.

As he walked back toward his house from the garbage can, where he'd deposited the unwanted bulbs, Andy *saw* the blood vessel break in his head. A brilliant flash behind his eyes, the clear sensation of something snapping. He slumped to the ground just outside his back gate. He opened his mouth to call for help – aware even at that moment of intense surprise that the only person near enough to hear him was the boy – and the pain in his head narrowed and sharpened as if it had been aimed. The reddening sun leveled into his eyes.

14

'Stroke,' said the doctor. This doctor was a huge man, dwarfing her father, who sat in his office chair. 'Cerebral vascular accident, actually. We refer to it as a stroke because its onset is so sudden that people used to say the victims had been attacked by the stroke of a fairy's wand.' He smiled, very slightly.

Breanne glanced at him sharply and, seeing no real amusement in his face, asked, 'What causes it?'

'A blood vessel bursts in the brain.'

Andy was nodding fiercely, and Breanne knew he was going to speak again.

Worst of all was the memory of her father lying crumpled in the mud with Greg standing over him in tears, like a victor or a protector. When she'd reached them, they'd both looked at her with terrified and, she swore, conspiratorial eyes. Almost as bad was her father's speech; the only thing apparently affected by the stroke after the first few hours of weakness and disorientation, his speech was only slightly fuzzy but nearly nonsensical. She braced herself and he said deliberately, 'I *caught* it.'

The doctor went on as if Andy hadn't spoken. 'Pressure builds up in the blood vessels of the brain and a hemorrhage occurs. Virtually any part of the brain can be damaged, affecting virtually any function. In your father's case, the damage has been done to the area controlling speech.'

'Will he get better?'

'Expressive aphasia is very difficult to treat. I will have my nurse refer you to a good speech therapist.'

'I like to *bargain* things,' Andy said, and Breanne saw his eyes flood with tears. Unreasonably, she was infuriated, as though once again her father was trying to foist on her something intimate and distasteful about himself, as in the forest confession of her girlhood – trying to give her something she dared not take or to take from her something she could not spare. He licked his lips and tried again. 'I like to *dampen* things.'

'*Discuss*,' she said, half under her breath, not knowing how she knew. 'He means *discuss*.'

'Emotional lability,' said the doctor kindly, 'is a very common side effect of a stroke. Patients often laugh or cry inappropriately.'

It was obscene for her father to be unable to control his emotions. It enraged her that she would have to start all over again, learning what she'd never learned in the first place – how to live with her father, how to guess what he meant, how to protect herself from him.

'How much – care will he need?' she asked.

Andy turned his head to look at her, tears glistening on his cheeks. She had, of course, never seen him cry before. The doctor clasped his hands around his knee and said, 'That depends. Right now I think he can probably function on his own, with a little supervision. There is no paralysis, and what weakness there is on the right side will probably improve with time. With expressive aphasics it's hard to tell, but I don't see any confusion beyond what we normally associate with old age. It's a vicious cycle, though, and it isn't always clear which comes first, the confusion or the inability to express oneself. It's hard to stay oriented when the words you hear yourself speaking aren't the words you had in your head.'

Andy fixed the doctor with a cold stare. 'I am not,' he declared, '*odor*.'

'Old,' she said. 'He means old.'

The doctor continued. 'The situation bears watching, however. Once someone his age has had a stroke, the chances of his having another one are greatly increased. It could be tomorrow, it could be ten years from now. You'll need to keep an eye on him.'

'Daddy.' In the neutrality of the doctor's office, with the large and official presence of the doctor between them, Breanne asked her father, 'Do you want to come live with me?'

Andy shook his head vehemently. 'Yes,' he said, and scowled.

'Aphasics often say the opposite of what they mean,' the doctor observed.

'But the words are clear. He can say the words.'

'Speech is a very complicated phenomenon. It's one of the major things separating humans from the lower animals. In this case what has been damaged is not the physical ability to form words but the connection between the message sent by the brain and the message received by the vocal apparatus. This particular kind of expressive aphasia is probably the most frustrating, both for the patient himself and for those around him.'

'Daddy,' said Breanne again. She had to fight the impulse to believe that he was doing this on purpose, taking one terrible step further his refusal to communicate with her on any but his own impossible terms. 'Do you want to live with Greg and me?'

Andy was still shaking his head, as if, once started, the motion could not be stopped. 'Yes,' he said emphatically. '*Yes*.'

Andy sat silently in his daughter's car and tried to name to himself the objects around him. Sky, he thought. Road. Car. Daughter. He knew if he tried to say the words something else would be spoken and he would not understand. No one would ever understand again. Rape, he thought, without pleasure. War. Cancer. Stroke.

He had not – even while it was happening, even while the boy stood over him – thought he was going to die. He had recognised it immediately for what it was. Loss of the power of words. All his life he had made things into what

86

they were not by naming them. Now, with the divine cruelty in which he had always secretly believed, he had been deprived not of the power of speech entirely, which would have been bad enough, but specifically of the power of naming. Now the anger would never get out into the world, because he could no longer name things for it to attack. He could feel it, loose inside.

Forgetting his new affliction even as he tried to talk about it, he turned to Breanne and said, 'I'm *thunderstorm* now,' and the instant the words were out of his mouth he had no idea what he had intended to say. The madness was already starting. The rage bellowed and butted in him like a caged bull. He gripped the armrest hard with his weakened right hand and left the other hand flat and white in his lap.

Breanne glanced at him and for a moment he was afraid she was going to pat his hand. Then he was thinking about Claire, his other daughter who had been gone so long he probably wouldn't recognise her on the street; about his little sister, Mary, whom he'd never see again. If she were still alive, she'd be old, like him and lonely. He gritted his teeth and wondered savagely whether the cerebral vascular accident had also destroyed his power to control his thoughts. If so, he might as well be mad, for it would be the same thing. 'Come have dinner at our house,' his daughter said to him. 'Then if you want I'll take you home.'

He nodded, and his head ached. It had not ached since the stroke. This headache filled him. It was black, and teeming with evil words. He doubted if it would ever go away. He nodded again, fiercely, and did not try to say a word.

Breanne put her arm around her father's waist to help him up the two low steps to the porch, but he shook her off and she reminded herself – watching him grip the rail as if, in fact, he was frail – that nothing but his speech had been affected. Nothing but his speech. The enormity of the damage was coming clear to her, the enormity of the change between them. She tapped at the door for Greg to let them in, but there was no answer. She fumbled her key into the lock, lifted the old door a little and pulled it toward her, and it opened. She ushered her father into her house, hung up their coats, and hurried into the kitchen, calling over her shoulder, 'Do you want coffee?' before she remembered that his answer, if it came at all, wouldn't be reliable. She didn't ask him again or go back into the living room where she could see him nod or shake his head; she just put the coffee pot on, irritably, and got out the kettle of stew.

Greg wasn't home. She knocked on his door and looked in – looked under the mounded covers and behind his closet door. She went to the back door and called his name. She was getting tired of this. She scanned the dining-room table for a note. He had gone somewhere again without telling her. It was nearly dark outside. He should be here, Breanne thought, in this house, a bright, warm, safe place like a Chinese box at the core of the layered night. Though she wasn't sure how safe it was anymore.

Breanne and Andy ate the stew and biscuits together, and hardly a word passed between them. By the time they had finished Greg was still not home. Breanne drove her father home and watched him let himself into his dark house. An old man, straight-backed, with something inside his head that had stolen his power to confer and hold names. He shut the door behind him and did not turn on the outside light, so she backed out of the driveway carefully in the dark and drove home. Greg was still not there.

She called his friends. One by one, no one had seen him. She called the police. They took his description, but he wasn't a missing person until twenty-four hours had passed and they wouldn't put out an alert. She sat by the phone, trying to think what else to do, and discovered that she was so tired that, like her father, she had lost the ability to name what was going on.

She went to bed and fell asleep – fell, rather, into a state of consciousness like a reflecting well, where everything echoed and she could not touch the sides. Greg was still not home, and she couldn't imagine where he was.

When she woke up – an hour, two hours, a lifetime later – something was *wrong*. She concentrated. Greg had run away. Her father had had a stroke. But something *else* was wrong.

She sat up. Something thick was oozing between her legs. Pain that while she slept apparently had floated throughout her body now plunged into her groin. And she was wet. Her legs were wet. Her buttocks were slimy. Her pubic hair was matted. Her thighs stuck to the sheet.

Blood. When she turned on the light she saw that her bed was pooled with blood.

Suddenly aware of how alone she was inside this house, inside all the layers of sleep and nighttime and power and anger in the world, Breanne stumbled down the stairs, pressing her nightgown up between her legs. By the time she got to the bathroom her nightgown was soaked. By the time she turned on the light and sat down on the toilet, her fingers were smeared with blood. And when she looked down, there in the bright-red water was something else. Something brown and spongy-looking; something, she thought in horror, shaped like a starfish or like a tiny human hand.

Breanne screamed. A small sound.

15

The emergency room was white and full of metal. Breanne lay on her back with her legs limply spread, under a paper sheet tented from the folds of its packaging, on a table so narrow that her knees and elbows kept slipping off. She was alone in a cubicle made of white curtains that were surely as insubstantial as the paper over her. The curtains stirred and parted every time somebody went by. People kept going by. White coats. A blue police uniform with silver flashing under the fluorescent lights. Somewhere nearby a man was mumbling hoarsely.

The pain came in waves, the blood in clots and spurts. Whenever the pain and the blood went away, Breanne slept. Dr Daniels wasn't here yet, though on the phone she'd promised to be. Breanne wondered whether doctors, like everyone else, could have perfectly coherent middle-of-the-night conversations of which they didn't remember a word. She wondered what it would be like to stay here unattended forever, and the fantasy wasn't entirely repellent.

It had seemed to take a long time for Dr Daniels to call back, although Breanne could see from the clock that it was only a matter of minutes since she'd placed her frightened, apologetic call to the answering service. She'd pressed her palm against the thick pad of towels between her legs and said shakily, 'I'm bleeding. Something's wrong. I'm bleeding a *lot*.'

'How much?' The doctor's voice sounded thick, and in

the background she could hear voices. She'd interrupted a party. It crossed her mind to apologise, but at the sound of the doctor's voice, the knowledge that here was someone to take care of her, panic had swept over her and her lips were trembling so that she could barely speak. She shut her eyes tight and imagined how she looked, face working grotesquely, blood seeping between her legs. She gasped at the image, and gasped again as pain clutched at her abdomen. 'How much blood, Breanne? It's important. Are you having to change your bed, say, every hour?'

'I'm not in bed,' she managed to say. Her teeth were chattering. 'I've got towels between my legs, and they're soaked.'

'Do you have pain?'

'Yes.'

'Severe pain?'

'Yes.'

'Are you passing tissue?'

'Yes.'

She heard a sharp exhalation. Then the doctor said gently, sternly, 'I want you to bring a tissue sample into the hospital. We'll need to run tests to see what it is.'

'I can't!' she cried, reaching behind her to flush the toilet again, although she had already flushed it a dozen times to get rid of the bloody water and the memory of the terrible jagged red-brown thing that had torn itself out of her. 'I can't! It's gone!'

'Go to the emergency room at Valley General,' the doctor said briskly. 'I'll meet you there in half an hour.'

'I'm – am I losing the baby?'

'We can't be sure until we examine you.'

'All right.'

'Half an hour,' the doctor said, and hung up.

'I should have saved the tissue,' Breanne said softly, but the line was dead.

She had driven herself to the hospital. She could have taken a cab, and she should have, but it didn't occur to her until she was halfway there, towels packed so thick under her that she was at a different and confusing angle to the pedals and the wheel; head swimming and eyes trying to focus on the nearly deserted city streets, which seemed to be wet and slippery although it hadn't been raining; mind skittering from the pain and the blood and the baby to the sudden, sharp, ridiculous fear that she would get a ticket for driving while having a miscarriage.

The lights in the hospital parking lot were blue and made a slight hissing noise in the night. Breanne opened the door and for a long moment found herself unable to get out of the car. Then she glanced around to make sure no one would see, surreptitiously adjusted the towels so they would stay between her legs, and hobbled to the emergency-room door. As the doors slid open, her fear hissed and shuddered and nearly pushed her back. Something terrible was happening to her baby.

It seemed a lifetime since she'd come here. She kept falling asleep, and every time she woke up her first thought was: Something terrible is happening to my baby.

The swarthy white-coated man who'd looked her over before now flung the curtain open and ushered Dr Daniels in as if he were escorting her to a ball. Breanne closed her eyes in relief and opened them again to the doctor's cool hand on her forehead, the doctor's high blond hair haloed by the bright lights behind her. She smelled of a subtle rose perfume, and she was wearing pale-blue eyeshadow above her pale-blue eyes. 'Breanne. How are you doing?'

'Okay. I'm still bleeding and still having cramps.' Where were you? Why have you made me wait alone in this alien and seductive place? But she couldn't organise her thoughts enough to ask, or even to be sure about the passage of time. All she knew for sure was the merciless emptying of her body, the filling of her mind with red pain.

'Let's have a look.'

Dr Daniels went to the foot of the table. The dark-skinned man followed, and Breanne heard him describing his earlier examination. She tried to understand his words, but at that moment the young man in what must have been the next cubicle bellowed, a series of metallic clatters echoed from the featureless walls, and someone shouted,

'Grab him! He's breaking the restraints!'

'Put your heels in the stirrups.'

She bent her knees wide and pushed herself down toward the end of the table, which she could not see. She was facing the gap in the curtains. Between her raised knees and between the heads of Dr Daniels and the emergency room doctor she could still glimpse forms moving, and voices from the other side of the curtain were clearer than her own thoughts. She flinched as Dr Daniels touched her labia, then tried to relax as the long fingers probed inside.

It seemed to take forever. It seemed to be over before she could make sense of it. Breanne's head was swimming. There was a rainbow haze around the tube of fluorescent light shining straight into her eyes. She balled her fist against her teeth and concentrated on keeping her stomach muscles relaxed.

Dr Daniels peeled off her glove, patted Breanne's knee, and pulled the paper sheet down. It tore. The doctor came to the head of the table and took Breanne's hand away from her mouth to hold it in both of hers. 'Your cervix is tight. I can't tell if you've had a miscarriage or not.'

'If I'd saved the tissue, could you tell?'

'Tests would have determined whether it was fetal tissue or just tissue from the uterine wall, yes.' Breanne sobbed, once, and turned her face against the doctor's hand. 'We'll schedule you for an ultrasound,' Dr Daniels went on hurriedly, gently, lifting her thumb to stroke Breanne's cheek. 'That will tell us what has happened.'

'Oh,' Breanne gasped, trying to catch her breath. 'When?'

'As soon as the hospital can get you in. It may be two or three days.' The doctor hesitated. 'It may be a week.'

'A *week*?' A week without knowing. A week with the pain and the blood – or with their memory, which might be worse. Breanne swallowed hard. 'What do you – suspect?'

'Don't, Breanne. There's no point in speculating –'

'*Tell me.*'

Dr Daniels sighed. 'I've had patients with trouble like this at four months go on to perfectly normal deliveries. I've had miscarriages, of course. And, of course,' she went on more slowly, 'we always have to worry about an ectopic pregnancy.' Breanne moved her head on the pillow to indicate she did not understand. She did understand, but she wanted the doctor to spell it out. 'A tubal pregnancy,' said the doctor. 'A fetus developing inside the Fallopian tubes.'

'The ultrasound would show that, too?'

'The ultrasound will show us exactly what's going on.'

'But a *week*. I don't think I can stand this for a week.' But of course she could.

'Call my office first thing in the morning and Nancy will get you scheduled.' Dr Daniels squeezed her hand and moved away, out of her line of vision. Breanne tried to sit up but couldn't find support on the narrow table and, for the moment, gave up. 'What I want you to do now,' the doctor's voice said, 'is go home and get some sleep. And try not to worry. Call me tomorrow and let me know how you're doing.'

Breanne thought about driving herself home, paying with the exact change to get out of the hospital parking lot, making turns, stopping for lights, parallel parking in front of her house, not knowing for a *week* whether she still carried the baby and whether it was alive or dead. She felt suddenly, acutely, abandoned. 'I thought you'd admit me,' she protested weakly. 'At least overnight. For – observation or something.'

'We seldom admit in cases such as yours,' Dr Daniels told her firmly. 'There's nothing anyone can do anyway, except watch and wait and keep your fingers crossed, and you can just as well do that at home. Do you have someone at home to take care of you?'

Breanne shook her head, wishing for her mother, who was dead.

The doctor sighed and patted Breanne's hair. 'Well, I want you to take it easy. Stay in bed as much as possible. Get a lot of rest. And call me. Whenever you think you need to, don't hesitate to call.'

Breanne nodded miserably and brought her knees up as pain washed over her. *Greg*, she thought, for the first time that night. *Greg*, and the pain touched places inside her body so private that she would have thought nothing and no one could reach them. It seemed clear to her that she was losing Greg, too.

The light hurt her eyes. The young man shouted again, wearily. The doctor was gone.

She did sleep, and she didn't dream, except for unattached snippets of dreams that didn't seem to mean anything. Everything else disappeared from her mind the moment she awoke, for her first waking thought was: Daddy-has-had-a-stroke-maybe-I'm-not-pregnant-anymore-Greg-is-gone.

A letter came from Jeff. Friendly, concerned, distant. He'd help if he could. ('I'll help pay for an abortion. I'll sign the papers to give the baby up for adoption.'), but refusing paternity. Years from now he could appear or she'd have to find some way of explaining him to her child. If there was a child.

She called her office and used up another sick day, knowing she had only two left. She sat up in bed, then slowly stood up, concentrating all her attention between her legs. There was no pain, no blood. Holding tightly to the rail, she made her way downstairs to Greg's room. She turned on the light, stepped over the piles of toys and clothes to look in the closet, patted the mound of sheets and blankets on the bed. Even softly called his name. Of course he wasn't there. She went to call Melinda.

'Lots of kids run when they feel themselves really getting close,' the social worker told her. 'How long have you had him now?'

'Almost nine months.'

'Did anything happen that might have precipitated this?'

'My father had a stroke.'

'Oh, Breanne, I'm sorry. Is it bad?'

'He has expressive aphasia. That seems to be the only damage. I don't know why Greg should run away over that. It certainly wasn't his fault.'

'Sometimes kids like Greg think everything's their fault. You told me that Greg and your dad don't really get along. Maybe secretly Greg wished something bad would happen to him, and now something has. Maybe he just couldn't stand tension in the family. Or maybe he didn't want to see you hurt.'

'Bullshit!' Breanne cried, suddenly so furious with Greg that she brought her fist down hard on the table, making her abdomen wrench. She tried to determine whether the vaginal blood was starting again, and couldn't. 'He doesn't care whether I get hurt or not! In fact, he deliberately makes things worse! And now I'm going to lose the baby, too! Maybe it's already dead!'

'What do you mean?'

'I'm pregnant. About four months. And I'm bleeding and I have terrible cramps and they won't know for three days to a week whether I've miscarried or the baby's dead *in utero*. And my father's had a stroke, and Greg chose *this* weekend to run away. *This* weekend. He *knew*, goddamn him, he *knew*.'

Quietly, firmly, Melinda said, 'I think I need to come see you this afternoon. Will you be home around four?'

'I can't go anywhere. I'm bleeding. But I'm not sure today's a good time to talk. You won't like the things I feel like saying today.'

'I'll be there at four.'

'Melinda.'

Breanne clenched her fist again and ran her knuckles across the table. The smooth surface was marred by tiny nicks, undoubtedly from Greg's pocket knife. Goddammit, she thought in outrage, goddamn him, *nothing* is safe from him.

16

That same morning Greg spent the last of his money on bus fare to the Social Services office. He wanted to wait until after nine o'clock, when the fare would go down, because then he would have enough left over for a pop, but he was afraid Melinda would be gone by then, out on home visits or court or to solve somebody's dumb problems somewhere away from the office.

He sat on the far back seat of the bus, across from the black dude with the orange stocking cap and the beady eyes who did some kind of card scam on the back of a ratty checkerboard spread across his knees. Greg swore he saw the same guy in the same stocking cap on half the buses he rode. He had listened to the patter lots of times and still hadn't figured out exactly what the game was. Now and then, when the eyes lighted on him, he'd been tempted to bet, but he never had been that stupid. He watched morosely as some old white guy laid down a five and, naturally, lost.

Greg had spent the night in somebody's garage around the corner from his house. Breanne's house. It was cold, and things kept moving in the dark. He thought they were rats or giant roaches or wild dogs; half a dozen horror movies played in his head so that he couldn't sleep. He'd watched the sun rise behind the downtown skyline and waited in vain for it to be spoiled by the brown cloud. He would have felt better if it hadn't been such a beautiful day.

He was tired. Tired of all this. Watching the gambler take another sucker, this one a young guy with a greasy ponytail who grinned while he lost what was probably the last ten-dollar bill he'd see for a while, Greg thought that he was like that with Breanne. A fool. A sucker. His real mom. His forever mom. Sure.

A scene like one of those horror movies with the rats and roaches slithered into his mind and he shook his head to make it go away, but it didn't. The old man saying that to him, she isn't your real mother, she'll never be your real mother, and Greg knowing it was true and knowing the old man was glad. Hoping the old man's head would blow up from one of his stupid fucking headaches, sitting inside the house and imagining a tiny explosion inside the old man's head, and then looking out the window and seeing him on the ground. Hesitating, his hand making prints on the big picture window. Running out the door and standing over the old man and seeing the recognition in the hard brown eyes. His mother finally showing up. Breanne showing up. Wanting to run to her and have her make it safe for him and knowing she couldn't, she wouldn't anymore, she had lied.

Well, it was all over now. The old man was sick, maybe dead. Standing over Andy and wanting desperately to help him but not daring to touch him, Greg hadn't needed a doctor to tell him what had happened. He could close his eyes and see the flash. He could feel the fury, stalking and clawing, trapped forever behind the set mouth and the buglike eyes.

And it was his fault. Oddly, unlike other times in his life when he'd done something wrong – though never anything as bad as this – he didn't know exactly how he'd done it. But Andy knew, and she would know. She was his mother.

Not anymore.

Greg watched a woman in a three-piece suit get off the bus. She glanced at the gambler and then looked away again, blushing. When the driver opened the back door and she started down the steps, she was peering at the gambler again and she almost fell. She was close to

Breanne's age. Under the brown skirt her stomach was flat. Greg thought clearly: *She's* not going to have a baby.

He had been thinking all night about the baby. Time after time he'd awake from a fitful doze, thinking rats were chewing on his shoes. He'd curl himself into a ball and then be thinking about the baby curled like that inside her. That close to her. That safe. He'd stand up on stiff legs, make his way through all the junk in the garage, and take a leak in the corner. Exposed and shivering, he'd be thinking about Debbie. Thinking about himself like a fish with eyes and a mouth and tiny little fingers, helpless in her womb like the pictures in the book. Helpless in her arms. Helpless in a bed where nobody came. Helpless when she gave him away. He'd scraped his hand on the cinder-block wall; it still hurt. He thought about Sherry.

Sometime in the middle of that night – because he couldn't sleep and the night was going on forever, because he was scared and he wanted to go home and he knew that he didn't have a home to go to anymore – he sat wide-eyed in the dark and constructed an elaborate fantasy. He pictured the baby in Breanne's womb, attached, breathing while she breathed, eating when she ate, moving everywhere she moved without even trying. He pictured it carefully, in red detail. Then he pictured it breaking. Something breaking. The cord snapping, the sac splitting open, the mushy baby's head flopping, the stuff around it that kept it safe tearing and leaking away.

He imagined it. He had a picture clearly in his head. He hugged his knees and pressed his back against the cold, rough wall, and was sure he heard the rats and the wild dogs everywhere. He thought about the baby exploding. He saw blood. He felt anger shooting through him like a drug.

But he knew it wouldn't work this time. She was too strong for him. The baby was too strong because it belonged to her the way he never would. He just had to go away.

And so, with the bright Monday morning sunshine and the first commuter bus, he was on his way to the social worker's office to tell her to take him away. He sat on the back seat and watched the black dude flip his cards, and tried again, half-heartedly, to figure out the game.

Before long Greg and the gambler were the only passengers on the bus. The gambler looked at him and kept up his quiet, quick patter. His long fingers skittered across the board. Like rats, Greg thought. He stayed where he was, scowling, his fists in the pockets of his jacket, his feet up on the sideways seat in front of him. Far ahead, over the rows of empty seats and through the tinted partition, he could see the back of the driver's head, and he imagined the brakes failing, the bus overturning, the black dude's fancy-dealt cards spinning all over the place. With a small sigh he put the image out of his mind before it got too real. There wasn't time for that now.

They went under the freeway and he saw the Social Services building up ahead on the right. He'd never come here on the bus before, but he had a good sense of direction and, though it looked like any of a hundred other buildings in the city – brown, square, with neat rows of windows, set in a concrete park – it was familiar to him. He had thought he'd never have to see it again. Fleetingly proud of his ability to get himself where he wanted to go without a mother or a social worker, he pressed the yellow strip that rang the bell and got up. As he stood on the back steps by the door waiting for the driver to pull into the stop, he glanced over his shoulder at the gambler, who was still watching him and still talking almost under his breath. Greg tried to meet the man's shifting eyes. As he jumped to the curb he could hear the clatter of the falling checkerboard and the gambler's cursing – still quiet, still singsong, as though it were part of his patter – as the cards flew to the floor. Greg allowed himself a very brief grin.

He pushed through the two sets of doors. He held his breath and tried not to smell, not to see, not to touch all the people waiting in the lobby. Barely eight o'clock in the morning and all these people waiting to get on welfare. He had an instant's comprehension of all the many variations of human need, but the understanding was more than he could take and he pushed it away with the thought of what he'd be doing right now if he were in school: Music class, Mrs Jacklin. He always got in trouble in music class.

Without looking at the receptionist or the long line in front of her, he crossed the lobby to the elevator and pushed the 'UP' button. The elevator came in a matter of seconds and there was no one else in it. He pushed the button for the third floor and slouched against the back wall, scowling as if someone could see him, feeling slightly sick.

'I need to see Melinda,' he told the fat lady at the desk.

'Is she expecting you?'

'No.' But she should be, he thought sullenly. She should be expecting me.

The fat lady looked at him with that mixture of curiosity and sympathy that always drove him crazy. Either she was a social worker, too, or she'd been around them too long. He gave her a dirty look but it must not have been a very good one because she didn't react at all — no smile, no fake understanding tilt of the head, no pursed lips. She just said, 'I'll see if she's in,' and went into another room.

Greg looked around the tiny waiting room, for the moment not knowing what to do. Then he sat down in one of the orange plastic chairs along the wall, tilted his head back, and thought how tired he was, how sick at his stomach.

'Greg.' He jumped. Melinda came out and stood in front of him with her hands in the pockets of her smock. She always dressed like a little kid, and she had long, straight, baby-fine hair, but he was not able to write her off entirely. For one thing, unlike other social workers he'd known, Melinda had so far always kept her word. Well, he had her this time, and he could hardly wait. He opened his eyes and gazed up at the ceiling when she said his name again. 'Greg. A lot of people have been worried about you.'

'So?'

'So what are you doing here?'

'Where else would I go?'

101

'Home.'

'That's not my home.'

'What's going on?'

'I don't know.'

'Bullshit.'

He heaved an exaggerated sigh. 'Okay, then. I don't want to answer that question. How's that?'

'Bullshit,' she said, surprising him again. 'That's why you're here. To answer that question.'

You think you're such hot shit, lady. You think you're so smart. But he followed her when she led him through a door into the inner hallway.

Just inside the door was a sign that said, 'Smile! Today is the First Day of the Rest of Your Life,' a sentiment which always filled him with a sense of dread. Melinda stopped and looked at him. It was a very narrow hallway and they were almost touching. He couldn't get far enough away from her, and so he met her eyes. Brown eyes, he noticed for the first time, but, unlike Andy's hard ones or Breanne's, which were kind of a golden brown, Melinda's were flecked with green. He knew his own eyes must be red-rimmed, and he concentrated on making them look as evil as he could. Evil. All-powerful. All-knowing.

'You look terrible,' Melinda said to him.

'You don't look so great yourself.'

'You look like you've been up all night.'

He shrugged. She looked at him some more, then turned left down an even narrower hall instead of right, which would have led to her desk in the big room with all the other desks. Wary, he followed her. She opened a door to a tiny room full of pillows. Pillows on the floor – big ones, little ones, all colors. Pillows on the walls, tacked on, glued on, making the room sound and feel funny around him. In roughly the center of the room was a stuffed dragon nearly as tall as Greg's waist, with four fat legs and a curled tail and a broad back you could probably sit on if you wanted to.

'What's this, the padded cell?'

'It's a place we can talk when we want some privacy,'

she said, and sat down among the pillows, pulling her ruffled skirt around her ankles and crossing her feet in brown high-strap sandals and white socks. She leaned one elbow on the dragon's back. 'It's a place for people to get really mad if they want to.'

'Well, I don't want to.'

She looked at him with those quick green eyes and said, 'Sure you do. That's why you're here.'

'Stop telling me what I'm thinking! You don't know what's in my head!'

'Why, Greg, of course I do. I'm a social worker, remember?'

'You're a mother-fucking bitch, that's what you are!' He was yelling. He was standing next to the door. He could have left. Instead, he kicked at a bright-yellow pillow shaped like a log and upended it. It gave and bounced back for more, so he kicked it again.

'And you're a scared little boy,' Melinda said deliberately, 'with delusions of grandeur.'

'What's that supposed to mean? Can't you speak English?'

'It means you think you control the world. You think you're so powerful that everything is your fault.'

'You're full of shit.' He picked up a square green pillow and threw it in her direction. It bounced off an orange beanbag and rolled over once.

'You think it's your fault your birthmom gave you up. You think you were abused because you're a bad person who deserved it. It seems to me you think mighty highly of yourself.'

Greg tried to kick a pillow in front of him. It squashed under his foot. The anger was swelling inside him like a balloon. He let himself imagine the social worker's little red heart exploding. Then he stopped the image and imagined instead that the pillows were bursting and their stuffing was all over the place. He imagined that hard, and at the same time his heel caught in the fringe of a huge flat black pillow and he fell. Caught off guard, he didn't get his hands up in time. His forehead hit the pillow and it hurt some and he swore. The seam of the pillow burst, letting loose a cloud of little foam curlicues.

The social worker sat with her hands clasped around her knees, watching him. 'You think if you'd been there you could have kept Sherry from dying.'

'Shut up!' Shut up, shut up, you're coming too close, you don't know what you're saying, you're in over your head. He threw a pillow at her. She caught it easily and threw it back. He threw himself face down among the pillows and fought with the pictures of rage inside his head as if they had tentacles. Clearly, he saw: Sherry's face, Andy's eyes, the inside of Breanne's womb. He was aware of trying to see Melinda's face, and aware that he could not.

'You think it's your fault that your grandfather had a stroke and that your mother might lose the baby.'

He stiffened. The baby. She was lying about the baby. But horrified, he knew she wasn't. The sickness he'd been feeling all day erupted and he thought he was going to throw up. He'd done it. He'd killed the baby. He hadn't meant to. The instant after he'd done it, he hadn't meant to.

Softly, Melinda said, 'You think if you give in to all that anger and really let yourself feel it, everything will blow up in your face. Don't you?' He was rigid, struggling to make his mind blank. She got up on her knees, put her hands on his cheeks, and forced his head toward her. *Don't you?*

'Get your filthy hands off me!' Her face floated behind his eyes but it stayed just out of reach.

Incredibly, she held on. 'Why should I?'

The fury swelled and rose like a poisonous balloon, and then with a rush of relief he let it go. It grew. Red and purple with stingers of black. It reached into parts of his body so private that he'd thought nothing and nobody could touch them. His fingertips blazed, his penis engorged, his hair stood on end, his heart ached. He screamed. He pounded his fists and kicked. He drew up his knees and forced them out straight, again and again and again. He sobbed and gagged and gasped for breath. He rolled over and tried to smother himself with the pillows, tried to stuff them into his mouth, then spat and hurled them away.

Desperately, he saw the square brown building bursting into flames, the neat rows of windows exploding outward and scattering sharp, shiny glass all over the place, the parking lot heaving and buckling, the whole city dancing in pain like hot popping corn, the whole earth tipping off its axis and spinning out of control.

None of it happened.

He didn't put the social worker's face in his mind. It was as if it wouldn't come. Later he would wonder what had kept it away, and what really would have happened if he'd seen her blood.

Melinda's arms were around him. She was lying on top of him, holding him down. He was crying like a baby now, almost unaware of how much time had passed or where he was or what had happened to him. She spoke into his ear. 'See, Greg? See? This is the worst it can get.'

17

Breanne poured Melinda another cup of coffee and, noticing that the social worker's hands were shaking, reached to touch her shoulder. It was an automatic gesture. She was not feeling sympathetic – to Greg or to Melinda or to anyone. She was furious, and exhausted, and, though there had been little pain and almost no blood this morning, afraid.

'He is,' said Melinda, 'the angriest child I've ever seen.'

'You're telling me.'

'I came out of that rage session with him feeling as if I'd been assaulted. My head hurt. My chest hurt. My back hurt.' She moved her shoulders tentatively and winced. 'Maybe it's just that he's getting awfully big to hold down.'

'He's gained seventeen pounds and four inches since he's been here.'

'That's not uncommon with our kids. Once they're in a stable home they start to grow physically as well as emotionally, and then they really make up for lost time.'

'I don't know how "stable" Greg's home is anymore, for any of us,' Breanne said. She crossed her legs and flinched at the tiny stab of pain to her groin – barely noticeable, really, except for what it might portend.

'Are you all right?' Breanne nodded. 'What happens next about the baby?'

'They've scheduled me for an ultrasound on Friday morning. Until then I won't know.' Breanne set her coffee cup down hard and bit her lip. 'I want you to keep Greg away from me until I know. I just can't handle him right now.'

Melinda shook her head. Light from the window behind her shadowed her face, and the tendrils of the spider plant – one of the few plants in the house that Greg had not broken or uprooted – made her features even harder to see. But Breanne could guess at the lift of the rounded jaw, the set of the green-flecked eyes. 'I don't think that's a good idea, Breanne. The more I work in this field the more I realise that a crisis isn't a good time to keep people apart. Usually they're so relieved that then they never want to get back together.'

'I can understand that.'

'That's what Greg said.'

'He did?' Breanne felt tears spring to her eyes and angrily refused to brush them away. They clung to her lashes and further blurred Melinda's dark form. 'What else did he say?'

'He told me to put him back in foster care. He said he didn't want to be adopted anymore. He said you wouldn't let him come back anyway after all he'd done. He said we might as well get this over with, because once the baby's born and you have your "own child," you'll send him away anyway.'

Finding it very hard to talk, Breanne said slowly, 'I just couldn't face him when you brought him home this morning. I was so relieved when you called and told me you had him, but by the time you got here with him I just couldn't face him.'

'That's probably just as well. He needed to be in school. Things need to be as normal as possible for him today. I just brought him by so he could get cleaned up. He was looking pretty scruffy from his night in your neighbors' garage.'

'I wonder what he destroyed in there.' Breanne laughed harshly. 'I'm sure I'll hear about it. Did he say anything about my not coming downstairs?'

'No. But we could hear you moving around and I

noticed that he kept looking up. Among other things, I'm sure he's worried about you and the baby.'

'That happened after he ran away. He doesn't know about the baby.'

Melinda groaned. 'He does now.'

'Wonderful. Now he's probably convinced himself that that's his fault, too.' Breanne shook her head. 'I know it's unreasonable, and I know he can't help it. I know he's been through a lot in his life, and it's a wonder he isn't more screwed up than he is. But I'm *sick* of his craziness, Melinda. I'm sick of trying to figure out the appropriate responses. I just want it to *stop*.'

Melinda nodded. 'I know. But it's not likely to stop for a while. He's got an enormous amount of rage. I don't think I realised just how much until I was alone in that room with him today. It was almost as if we *weren't* alone, you know? As if his anger was a presence, a power, in its own right.'

Breanne swallowed. 'I've felt that, too.'

'If it's that strong and that scary for us, imagine what it must be like for him. Kids his age engage in magical thinking anyway, and there must be times when it feels like a supernormal power to him.'

'Melinda,' Breanne heard herself saying. 'What if it is?'

'What if it is what?' she social worker asked, so sharply that Breanne guessed the thought had crossed her mind, too.

'Supernormal.'

'Well, in a sense it is. I mean, rage like this may be logical and expected in a kid with a history like Greg's, but you certainly can't call it "normal." ' She hesitated. Breanne couldn't tell if she was looking at her or not, but she had the sensation that Melinda's eyes, usually so direct, were uneasily focused somewhere else. 'I'm sure when you're around it all the time it must seem pretty awesome.'

'I just get so tired,' Breanne said.

'Can you get away much?'

'I go to work.'

'How often do you take an evening just for yourself?'

'Not often,' Breanne admitted. 'I guess I'm afraid to leave Greg alone, even though he should be old enough. And it always made me nervous to leave him with Daddy, which of course isn't possible anymore anyway.' She laughed, still an angry sound even to her own ears. 'Besides, the last time I took an evening for myself I got pregnant.'

'That is not,' Melinda said, also with a forced little laugh, 'necessarily a logical consequence.'

Breanne said nothing. For an instant she had imagined there was movement in her belly, but she knew that couldn't be so. The sensation was gone almost at once, leaving her bereft.

'You need to take care of yourself,' Melinda said gently. 'I'll be glad to help you find a sitter, if you like.'

Breanne nodded.

'We have some people who know about angry kids. Although I do think Greg and I got somewhere today. I goaded him until he really lost it, and of course the world didn't blow up around him. Literally or figuratively. I think he needed to have that demonstrated.'

'That's good.' Breanne's spine was still tingling, her mind still cavorting around some thought that she couldn't pin down.

Melinda glanced at her watch. 'It's about two o'clock. What time does Greg get home from school?'

'Two thirty.' Noticing that her hands were pressed protectively across her stomach, Breanne moved them to the arms of the chair. 'I appreciate your changing your schedule to be here. I have no idea in the world what to say to him.'

'What do you *want* to say to him?' Melinda shifted position and the longest stem of the spider plant swayed behind her. 'Do you want to tell him to leave? Do you want to disrupt? Because if you do, I'll help you find a way to say it –'

'No! Stop it!' cried Breanne, and burst into tears. Then, as abruptly, she stopped crying, pulling the sobs painfully back into her throat, afraid of her own fear.

Melinda was at her side, sitting on the arm of the chair, lightly hugging her, and the sensible lines and planes of her face were reassuringly back in the light. 'I know it isn't an easy thing to think about. But it'll only get harder the longer you have him. I want you really to think about it, Breanne. I want you to consider whether the price of keeping him is too high.'

Obediently Breanne took a deep breath and tried to consider. She thought about disrupting the adoption. She thought about sending Greg away. She thought about saying to herself and to him and to the world that there was no longer any connection between them.

And simply could not.

'No,' she said, relieved, and felt Melinda's fingers tighten a little on her shoulder. 'No. He's my son.'

18

'Greg,' said Breanne sharply, 'there's nothing you can do about this.'

He looked at her, and she realised with a little shock how seldom he looked at her like that – directly, without the sensation that he was slipping and sliding away.

'There's nothing you can do about the baby. This is not in your control. You can't make anything happen or not happen.' She stopped, then sighed. 'Neither can I. All either of us can do is wait.'

He nodded. It was Tuesday evening. They had already made it through twenty-four hours of waiting together. Breanne had had no more pain or blood, but her muscles were straining from holding herself ready for a renewed attack. Greg, she could tell, was waiting, too. He was always waiting for something, but this seemed to be different. Instead of waiting for the right moment to take action himself in a crazy attempt to control an uncontrollable world, this time he seemed to be waiting for something to happen *to* him, and there was a feeling of relief about him, almost of peace.

And between them was a knowledge that hadn't been there before, as if this time they really were touching each other, and holding on.

He was doing the dishes. She had assigned him the dishes – his most loathed chore – to pay back at least symbolically the time and energy she'd spent worrying about him while he was gone. He'd been grumbling and muttering to himself, but when she went in and sat on the high gray kitchen stool, he grinned at her over his shoulder, his arms up to the elbows in soapsuds that flecked and foamed against his dark skin. From the looks of it he'd used half a bottle of detergent, but she decided not to say anything.

'Listen,' she said. 'Let's not tell Grandpa about the baby.'

'Why not?'

'Not until we know something. He'll just worry.'

'So? You're worried. I'm worried,' he added a muffled voice as he turned away from her to pick up another precarious stack of dishes. He dropped it from a dangerous height into the water, causing his mother to wince and the soapy water to splash into his own face. 'Shit,' he said, and glanced at her guiltily, although she'd never made an issue about his language, which, in any case, was no worse than her own.

'Yes,' she said, 'but Daddy's not very good at worrying.'

'You don't like him.'

'No, I don't. Although,' she said, surprising herself a little, 'I think that's starting to change.'

'How is he, anyway?'

Breanne sighed, feeling for the first time since her father's stroke a real sadness for him, a real grief. 'Oh, I don't know. Physically he's okay, I guess. The stroke only affected his speech.'

'You mean he can't talk at all?' Greg's brown, long-lashed eyes were wide over the plate he was drying.

'He can talk. But the words he says aren't the words he means.'

He stopped drying and was staring at her as if in disbelief. 'What do you mean?'

'Oh, he'll mean to say he's *tired*, for instance, and it'll come out that he's *thunderstorm*.'

'Thunderstorm?' Greg guffawed. 'That's weird.'

'It must feel pretty weird from the inside,' she said pointedly.

'Yeah.'

112

There was a pause. He scrubbed at a pan. Finally she asked, 'How was school today?'

'Fine.'

'You still getting along okay with Mr Franconi?'

'He's okay.'

Once, in tears over her insistence that he had to do what Mr Franconi told him to do, Greg had yelled at her that she had no idea what school was like for him, how awful it was all the time, how he suffered. Even granting his pre-adolescent penchant for melodrama, she guessed that was true. She wanted to understand, but he wouldn't let her in.

Now she stirred on the hard stool and stretched her hands over her head. 'I'm tired.'

'Me, too. I'm real thunderstorm.' He giggled. 'And I got homework.'

She raised her eyebrows. 'What brought this on?'

'Nothing.' He scowled and pulled the plug out of the sink with a dull, sickly pop.

With the exaggerated care that had become habit lately, stemming, no doubt, from her new awareness of how fragile everything was – her body, her relationships, life itself, her warm safe core at the center of a windy night when the moon was in eclipse – Breanne stood up. Something in her pelvis ached for a split second, then subsided as if it had never been there. 'I've got homework, too,' she said. 'Reports due this week that I'm real behind on.' And couldn't restrain herself from adding, 'I seem to have had a little trouble concentrating lately.'

Greg flung the wet dishtowel at the macramé-owl towel rack Breanne's mother had made for her years ago. It caught and held by one corner. 'Shit,' he said. 'I hate dishes.'

He tried to do his homework. It was math, his worst subject, and he tried to make sense out of the fractions, but, as usual, it was so hard for him to concentrate that at times the stupid numbers actually seemed to jump around and disappear from the page. When they did that they were, of course, no use to him at all.

He laid his head on his desk in the flat funnel of light and thought that it was the same way with his anger. Carefully, allowing himself, he thought about what he'd learned in the social worker's padded room.

He knew it wasn't what she thought he had learned. He knew she didn't understand him. No one did. Not Melinda, who thought she knew everything about abused and neglected kids. Not Mr Franconi, who talked about hormones as if they were little monsters running around inside his pants. Not Breanne, his mother for sure now although he didn't understand why, who made him feel both safe and scared. They each understood a piece of it. They each had an idea. But like the blind men and the elephant – a story he'd read the other day in English class, of all places, amid all the shit about gerunds and participles, and it had stuck with him – like the blind men and the elephant they never saw the whole truth. They only saw what they wanted to see. They didn't see *him*. There was pride in that.

In the room full of pillows, he had thought about the world blowing up, and it hadn't. He had pictured the building going up in flames, and it hadn't. Ever since he'd been aware of the rage inside him, he'd thought he had to control it, to sit on it, because if it ever got loose something huge and horrible would happen. In that room it had gotten loose, and nothing at all had happened.

So now he understood. His anger was a tool. In order to use it he had to concentrate. In order to make anything break he had to be able to hold a picture of it in his mind. Diffuse anger – Melinda had said the words, and he'd made a point of remembering them – wouldn't cut it. Anger itself was nothing to be afraid of. His power hadn't left him, nor had he imagined it in the first place. It was real. It was his. It was to be used and refined.

Breathless, Greg sat up. He was thinking about Andy. He realised a little fearfully that already he knew more about life than the old man did. Andy had spent his life denying the rage, and so he had denied the power. And what did he have to show for it? Greg recited the list to himself like a lesson. Headaches. A dead wife. One kid he never saw and another who didn't like him. A stroke, which had left him saying things he didn't mean. It wasn't clear to Greg exactly what all these things had to do with Andy's bottled-up rage, but at that moment he was awash with his first adult realisation of what it can mean to miss an opportunity.

He decided to test himself. He closed his eyes and thought about a hole in the plaster of his wall, just above his Stray Cats poster, and when he opened his eyes a tiny hole had appeared. It could have been there before, but he was sure it hadn't been. He gazed at the shirt hanging from the doorknob of his closet and imagined the threads popping that held on the second button. When after a few minutes he hadn't heard the button *ping* onto the floor, he went over to examine it, and sure enough the button was gone. He sent a shot of pain down into his own foot, flinched, and stopped it before it did any real harm.

It wasn't true that he could do nothing about the baby. Breanne didn't understand him either – but then, he told himself almost serenely, he didn't really expect her to. She had her own kind of mysterious power, a mother's power, and he could accept that now. He had his own. If he thought about it, if he knew exactly what was wrong, he could do something about it. He could break the tube, push the baby back inside something. What he lacked was knowledge, and now he saw how important knowledge was. Maybe he would be a doctor when he grew up. Maybe he would be a writer, naming things, breaking them apart into words.

Feeling a little giddy, he tapped his pencil against his teeth and stared again at the much-folded and palely mimeographed homework paper. 'Reduce to the lowest common denominator.' He frowned. He squinted. On an impulse he tried concentrating on the problem using the technique he had just been testing. He thought of the power in a thin, straight line. He pictured the fractions breaking, breaking down, literally and concretely reducing to the lowest common denominator.

He bent over the paper and one by one wrote down the answers, pressing so hard and so steadily that the point of the pencil dulled and the answers came out heavy and shiny and black.

It occurred to Andy that he might be preparing for death. It wouldn't surprise him to die. He was seventy-four years old, and he had had a stroke. Death could come at any time.

What did surprise him were two things: The fact that he did not want to die and the fact that he was actively preparing for it. Reviewing his life. Setting his life in order. *Remembering*.

'Don't cry. Big boys don't cry.' His mother lying flat and sweet in the coffin, his father with the prickly beard in the coffin next door, his big brother John with his eyes closed forever. Andy stood in the church, wearing the hand-me-down suit that John used to wear to church on Sundays, Mary beside him, her thumb in her mouth; she'd kept trying to hold his hand but he wouldn't let her, he kept flinging her hand away. The church was hot. The organ music filled his head and made him dizzy. All around him were people he didn't know, crying. He didn't cry. Not one tear. All the tears stayed inside.

Now, sitting in the rocking chair with Ruth's hard pillow behind his neck, comforting even though he didn't have a headache – he had had very few headaches worth mentioning since the stroke, and that, oddly, was a loss – now, Andy cried. He sat in his chair with his neck pressed back against the hard pillow and his eyes wide open watching the birds at the birdfeeder and in his mind putting words to them – grackle, chickadee, jay. It startled him that the words still formed themselves in his mind as clearly as if he had some use for them. He cried. For all the things he had lost in his life. For all the things he had never had. For all the things he would never have now, if he was going to die.

He sat and cried and named the birds in his head, and the power of the grieving amazed him. Unfamiliar with weeping, he wondered if it would release the sadness and anger from him, rob him of them as the stroke had robbed him of the spoken word, and then, he wondered, what would be left of him? Without sadness and anger and words? Nothing. A hollowing out. A preparation for death.

A huge blue-black grackle hopped onto the birdfeeder amid a flock of small fat chickadees. They fluttered, re-arranged themselves, and went back to their seed. The sun was setting among the pines on the other side of the valley. It was Wednesday afternoon. Crying hard, his nearly toothless mouth open wide and sounds coming from it that he would not have recognised, Andy found himself thinking about the boy. Frightened by the utter irrelevance and intrusiveness of it, he pushed the face away.

He remembered. He remembered Claire. He remembered what she'd said to him the last time they'd talked, her words coming at him like bullets over the phone. 'You don't *say* things, Daddy. I've never heard you say to anybody, "I think you're right," or, "I never thought of that" or, "You did a good job" or, for that matter, "I love you." When was the last time you told Mom you loved her? He had not hung up. He had listened infuriated by her insolence and her stupidity, and after awhile he had simply handed the phone to Ruth.

Claire, his firstborn. Claire, whose terrible colic pains had eased only when he held her against his stomach, her soft head scant inches away from the point of his chin, her bootied feet not quite touching his lap. In whose tiny face he had seen such need for him that he could not begin to name it, and, later, revulsion so huge that there had been no name for it, either.

Now he could not name anything aloud. He moved his head in anguish on Ruth's pillow. When had words become so important to him, anyway? Why should this be a loss for him to mourn, like all the others? He had wanted to be a musician, not a writer. With a sensual rush in his chest and the tips of his fingers, he remembered how music had underscored and elucidated and in fact created the important things in his life, things for which there never were any words.

He forced himself to think words. Cancer. Delinquency. Herpes. AIDS. Trapped inside his head they had, of course, lost their glory, but they retained some of their old ability to satisfy, to keep at bay the things they named. Claire, as usual, was wrong. He'd said a great many things in his life. Now he would be able to say no more.

He stood up and walked to the window, noticing the evening light. The birdfeeder was empty now, and he had not seen the birds fly away. He thought he could hear a chickadee trilling somewhere and in his mind vividly saw the plump black-and-white body among the frothy branches of a pine. Before long it would be summer, and the birds wouldn't need handouts any more, although if he kept putting it out, they'd keep taking it, as if they were doing him a favour. Yellow and red and salmon-colored roses were blooming beneath the window; they bloomed every year.

Ruth. He thought her name like a pistol shot, and all the anger from all the years of living with her, all the love, assaulted him. Ruth. There were streaks on the windowpane. Except for the meals Breanne brought him once or twice a week – covered dishes that looked and tasted like nothing her mother had ever made – he ate from cans and boxes. His clothes were wrinkled, and half a dozen pairs of underwear had turned mottled pink when he'd washed them with bright-red socks.

He missed Ruth. It was not just the comfort and orderliness he missed, the activities of daily living she took care of. It was the overall feeling of safety. Alone now, he was endangered. He couldn't protect himself. He was an old man. He had read somewhere that single men over sixty-five have the highest suicide rate in the country, and he knew why. If he'd never loved her, he wouldn't have been put in this position. It outraged him. Love, he thought, and thought it again to keep it away. Love. Ruth.

'She stood in tears amid the alien corn.' He remembered the line with the cold pleasure poetry always gave him, so unlike the hot and dangerous joy he'd felt a long time ago, playing his horn. He believed in poetry as an art form and a ritual, meant for keeping emotion under control, and, in the hands of the masters, it worked. Keats had, of course, been talking about the biblical Ruth, but his Ruth, too, would have followed him anywhere if he'd let her, would have tried to take his people as her own, would always have shed tears for him no matter how long they had lived together – and would always have remained a stranger.

Andy had spent much of his life making sure he was a stranger in the world. His interior landscape was so dark and treacherous and full of furious alien life forms that any real passage to and from the outside world had to be constantly sealed. He knew what lived in there. Loneliness, terror, rage. It had taken a lifetime to catch up with him – a human lifetime, paltry in the cosmic scheme of things, to be sure, but now to him precious and immense. It had taken his lifetime, but now he knew that the things trapped inside him would have their way with him at last, would kill him.

To his surprise Andy regretted that, and in the silence of his dusty house he cried out. He paced. He turned on the radio, heard the tinny sound of someone else's voice, turned it off. He watched the spring night fall.

It had something to do with the boy. The realisation came on him with such force that he reeled under it, clutching the back of a chair. His head pounded. The boy was at the root of this. It was the boy's fault.

Andy went into the guest room – kept straight all these years by Ruth and untouched since her death except by the settling dust. He found, in the desk drawer where they had always been, a stenographic notebook and a blue Parker pen. He carried them back to his rocker, turned on the light, sat down. Putting pen to paper, he began furiously to write things down.

He'd show them all what his words could still do. The words that appeared on the bluish half-pages constituted a message. They were, in fact, the words he meant to write. He did not know whether they were the right words, the words that could bring the boy to him, teach him a lesson, and then send him flying away again forever. Andy gritted his teeth.

Breanne said, 'He's a different person.'

Getting ready for school on Thursday morning, Greg heard her through the heat register. Yesterday he'd re-arranged his room, taking extraordinary pleasure in pushing his bed to the middle of the room instead of against the wall where she'd had it, in collecting and throwing out the shattered pieces of his dresser (he didn't need a dresser anyway; he had three red oval clothes baskets), in hanging up his Rambo poster and his Garfield beach towel. Moving the bed exposed a heat vent in the wall, smaller than the one in the floor that his heat came through. Through it he could hear – echoey, slightly distorted, but perfectly easy to understand – anything Breanne said in the room upstairs.

He was sure that Breanne knew. She knew lots of things. When she came in to admire his room's new look he expected her to say something about the register, or at least to glance at it in that straight-faced way that meant she'd noticed something he hadn't wanted her to notice. But she didn't. She exclaimed about his room, commented on the Black Stallion jigsaw puzzle he'd done at the Garcias' when he was eight and Mrs Garcia had helped him spray-glue onto a piece of cardboard and three or four pieces were missing now, leaving holes in the stallion's ear and tail. She didn't say anything about the register. He was pleased with himself and also a little discomfited by this further evidence that mothers didn't know everything.

He wondered who she was talking to on the phone about him so early in the morning. Her voice was a little muffled but he could make out almost every word, even while he zipped his pants and laced his shoes. 'The tension is almost gone. The explosiveness is gone. Well, not gone exactly, but different somehow. Less crazy. Less dangerous. Or maybe I'm just getting used to it.' Pause.

'Well, I don't know what you two did in that rage session, but something has definitely changed.'

Melinda. He'd never actually heard them talk about him before. It was a creepy feeling, like looking at yourself in a mirror when you first wake up. He listened carefully.

'Of course, it's only been a few days. But maybe he's finally got all that anger out of his system.'

Greg shivered. He almost laughed aloud. These two women, so powerful to him, didn't know shit this time about what was going down with him. They'd missed it. They'd guessed wrong. Something *had* happened to him in the room with the pillows, but it couldn't be much further from what they thought it was. The tension wasn't gone. The anger wasn't 'out of his system.' If anything, it was *in* his system, really, for the first time. The anger was in him now like blood, like air. Now he knew what it was for. Like the beating of his heart. Breanne and Melinda didn't know. He shook his head in amazement. He was safe. He was alone.

'I feel okay,' Breanne was saying. 'The test is tomorrow. It's been a long wait. For both of us, I think.'

Greg began to gather his homework from his desk, wondering what time it was. Two watches, one of them a digital he knew must have been expensive, had broken since he'd been here, and Breanne said she wouldn't buy him another one for a while, until he could take care of it. She thought he was careless. She thought his curiosity and his destructiveness sometimes got mixed up. She'd told him that. He grinned. She didn't know the half of it. Nobody did. Not even Andy. Greg himself was just beginning to learn.

He glanced quickly over the science homework. It looked right to him. Since he'd discovered he could use the power on schoolwork he hadn't, to his disappointment, suddenly started getting straight As, but things were easier, clearer, and he felt less hopeless when he looked at a book. Mr Franconi wasn't saying all the time anymore, 'You're just not living up to your potential.' School would be out in another couple of months, and he'd have the summer to practice. Greg pushed the papers into his folder, uncovering the book he'd hidden underneath.

It was the book about embryos and fetuses and babies. Greg slid his hand across the cover and said the words in his mind: 'Embryo. Fetus. Baby.' He'd taken the book from the bookshelf in the living room, and Breanne must have noticed. That bugged him. She'd think he was just looking at the pictures, 'dealing with' the idea of having a baby, and he *was* doing that. He was also doing something more organised and deliberate, and much more important.

Quickly he flipped through the pages. There it was, head like a tulip bulb, the beginnings of toes and fingers, umbilical cord disappearing off into some kind of murky stuff that sent a chill down Greg's back. He stared at the picture. He imagined a power like his developing in the tiny brain. He knew it was. For with growing maturity had come to Greg an understanding that everybody had power. Everybody could, in some way, break things or change things or make things happen. It was a matter of taking charge of what was inside you, the good and the bad, the fear and the love and especially the anger. Greg now believed that everybody had that kind of anger, and that in fact you probably couldn't live without it. When he was little he used to be convinced that there was nobody else like him in the whole wide world. Now he saw the power in everybody; it was just that most people refused it, or didn't know it was there.

He traced the outline of the fetus's outsized head and thought about Breanne going in for her test. The name for it was ultrasound. Tomorrow they would find out what had happened to the baby. Ultrasound found out things by piercing through flesh and leaving no trace, causing no damage, hurting no one. Greg liked that.

If the baby was dead, there would be nothing he could do about it. It was hard for him to admit that, even to himself, but it was true. Everybody's power had limits.

If the baby was trapped inside one of those tubes – *Fallopian tubes*, he said carefully to himself, suspecting there was power in naming; *ectopic pregnancy* – then there was a lot he could do. His power was breaking things. Setting things free. He could barely contain his excitement, just thinking what a neat thing he could do for Breanne, and she wouldn't even know it was him.

Then the baby would be born. It would be a perfect baby, and it would be hers. Then she wouldn't want him anymore. Greg knew how that worked. He would go away. It wouldn't be the first time he'd been sent away. This time he would know why. This time, he would know what he'd done to cause it. This time he would be in control.

'Greg!' Breanne called down the stairs, and with a start he realised she was off the phone. He frowned. He would have to pay more attention, get control of himself. Live up to his potential. All the things adults had been telling him for as long as he could remember, and now he saw that they'd been right, though not in the way they'd meant. 'Greg, it's eight fifteen.'

'Okay.' He shoved the book far back in his desk drawer, picked up his homework folder, and clattered down the stairs.

Breanne jumped at the cold touch of the conductive jelly on her abdomen, though the technician had warned her. She was scared. She said out loud, 'I'm so *scared,*' and immediately felt the panic worsen.

The technician, a lank-haired, flat-cheeked woman in her thirties, obviously misunderstood. 'Nothing to it,' she said, kindly but irrelevantly. 'It won't hurt.'

Breanne turned her head and across the room caught Greg's eye. He was looking embarrassed, and she knew it was the sight of her stomach, bared from just below her breasts to just above her pubic hair, obviously swollen. He looked frightened, and she knew he was, like her, frightened of the instruments and the procedure and the shining room, and of the news, whatever it was, that they were about to hear. He looked proud and she guessed, with a degree of pride herself, that it pleased him to be part of this adult event. And he looked – enraged? That wasn't quite the right word anymore, though rage was still the first emotion she thought of when she looked at him. Intense? Focused – the way sunlight can be focused through a magnifying glass to burn.

The word that came to her then was *empowered*, but she didn't know why. Suddenly she feared it had been a mistake to have him here.

'Now,' the technician said, and below Breanne's feet something clicked. A monitor like a TV screen switched on in the facing wall, and the technician reached toward Breanne's belly with a round metal object in her hand. 'This is the transducer. It will pick up whatever is in the uterine cavity.'

The transducer made contact with the jelly spread across Breanne's skin, and almost at once an image appeared on the screen. Greg gasped. Breanne stared. It was hazy, a hodgepodge of grays. There was nothing she dared to define – eyes, arms, toes – and for a terrible instant she thought she was seeing the empty inside of her own uterus, perhaps still littered with the tissue and blood her body had prepared for the baby, but otherwise and truly empty.

She closed her eyes and opened them again when the technician said in a voice as lank and flat as the rest of her, 'There it is.'

'What?' Breanne asked stupidly.

'The fetus.'

And Breanne saw it. Or thought she saw it. Like looking for meaningful patterns in inkblots or clouds, she thought: You could see what you wanted to see.

'The black is the amniotic fluid,' the technician said conversationally, running the instrument across Breanne's abdomen again and producing another flickering image. 'The lighter area is the baby.'

It was an eerie feeling, actually and physically to be peering inside herself. It made her want to stir self-protectively on the table, to hide herself and the baby, to close herself against prying and danger, against Greg. But she lay still, afraid to disturb the picture on the screen, more afraid of adding something – some movement, some

124

evidence of life – that wasn't really there.

The transducer in the technician's hand moved again, and the image on the screen fluttered. 'What does it mean?' Breanne asked carefully. 'Does it mean I haven't miscarried? The baby's still alive?'

But before the technician could answer, Greg was on his feet and pointing. 'There's the heartbeat! See it?'

And Breanne – propped on her elbows now to peer over the slight hump of her stomach where the baby was – saw it. A tiny but unmistakable and regular pulsing in the area of the monitor screen that was lighter than the rest. She saw it. Like a trapped bird. Like a bird held safe until it was ready to fly. Like nothing, really, but what it was: Her child, as truly as Greg was hers, alive inside her in a place she had never really known existed. A baby, growing, waiting to be born. Her baby's strong heartbeat, and her own furious joy, and Greg staring and pointing with a look on his face for which there was no name.

19

It was May. Corn was coming up in backyard plots and in the narrow strips of dirt between sidewalk and street. Greg noticed the pale-green corn and the squash rines beginning to twist among the stalks. Later in the summer, he knew, he would eat four or five or six ears at a sitting, the corn every bit as sweet in the crowded city air as in the pure country, and by September Breanne would be baking acorn squash with sausage and cinnamon.

When Andy came into town, he glanced at the corn and squash and at the rows of lettuce crooked around the stop signs and the tree roots, and he scowled at them. To Breanne the gerrymandered little gardens seemed absurd and terribly brave, and with pleasure she kept track of their considerable productivity. That summer it seemed to her that bravery and usefulness often developed in the face of patent absurdity, where you would never have expected them to flourish.

The sky was blue and cloudless day after day, slightly paler blue over the mountains, a dusty blue-brown over the city center and the interstates. Tiger lilies were spiking around the front of the house. Along the outside wall of Greg's bedroom the irises were covered with fat pink buds that for weeks had looked as if they could burst any minute. From his first summer there Greg knew that when they opened it would be one or two at first, like advance scouts, and then all at once, fall and bright like flags. Some people called them flags instead of irises. Greg remembered that, and was pleased that he had a history in this place.

Breanne was six months pregnant, and showing. Andy didn't like to look at her, but he did, and whenever he looked he saw something different. His daughter about to bear his grandchild, that simple. A girl in trouble, more trouble than she knew. A woman who was not Claire or Ruth or his mother – and he remembered each of them pregnant, and married, and vulnerable. And each of them had set him aside – his mother had been pregnant again when she died. His grown daughter. A woman who didn't know her place, though since she was a baby he'd tried to teach it to her. Who paid more attention to the boy, who was already formed beyond any hope of change – anyone who was at all well read in psychology knew that personality is formed within the first six months of life – paid far more attention to the boy than to him or to the child in her womb. A link to the mysterious life forces of the universe which Andy was beginning to apprehend in a way that suggested they had been there all the time. An insignificant speck in the vast, chaotic, indifferent scheme of things.

Heroin addiction, he thought clearly, for he was convinced she didn't know who the father was. Stillbirth. And, for some reason, missing link. He sat in his chair and wrote everything down, and often he went to bed exhausted, without remembering to eat.

Breanne was seldom sick anymore, though once in a while a whisper of nausea would slither through her stomach and make her think in despair that the worst of it might be coming back. The fatigue had eased, too, so that now, on eleven or twelve hours of sleep, she could function for the rest of the day. There had been no more blood and only nondescript twinges of pain. Every two weeks Dr Daniels still cautioned her to take it easy, not to overdo. 'The only successful treatment we have for this kind of problem pregnancy is bedrest.' But Breanne guessed from the doctor's almost-casual, almost-hurried manner that the pregnancy was now proceeding routinely. Often now she felt the baby move.

Breanne was alive with such peace, such joy, that it was easy for her to believe that Greg felt the same way. Yet she would waken in the night, almost every night, trembling with the terrible dream – and, for long moments, a waking dream – that somehow her baby would not be born, and she would hear Greg moving inside his room, climbing the stairs, standing outside her door.

Greg played that he made the baby move. During the day – at breakfast when she was wearing her robe, after dinner when they did the dishes together and she couldn't get close to the sink and they would giggle together at the weird way she had to stand – he would glance at her belly and feel a hot rush of amazement at the evidence of new life there. At night he dreamed about it, about his power over it, and woke up with a hard-on, and couldn't stay in bed.

He didn't think about the baby *all* the time. He didn't need to. He played ball with his friends. He went to the movies. He thought about Maria, who sat in front of him in Mr Franconi's class; he wrote her name on his arm. Then, like a game, he'd think about the baby – the *fetus* – safe inside Breanne the way he had once been safe, and gently he'd imagine what it looked like now, and exactly how and where it was attached, and in his mind he'd move it around a little and play that it was actually physically moving, upstairs in Breanne's room, under the covers, inside her body, inside her uterus, inside all the blood, the baby was really moving because he wanted it to. Then he would catch a high fly, or write Maria's phone number on the wall over his bed, or fall asleep.

Breanne went to work every day and picked up a few new clients, one of whom had enough money and enough fluid assets at his disposal to make things interesting. She was excited again by the vagaries of the market – which were at heart satisfyingly unpredictable, despite all the handy indicators they'd taught her in grad school. She was fascinated by the perturbations of the banking and investment industry. Various combinations of abstract numbers excited her in ways they hadn't for years. During that summer she made the biggest commission of her career, and her wealthy freewheeling client, in a fit of jubilation, proposed marriage. She declined, and instead he expanded his portfolio with her.

School ended. Every day Greg got up after Breanne left for work, fixed his own breakfast, did his dishes. He watched cartoons for a while in the morning, or read another science-fiction paperback, or experimented with a recipe for molasses and peanut butter cookies or a new way to fry potatoes. Around eleven he usually went over to Pete's or Cameron's, where they played the Atari, and then they went to the Boys' Club to swim or up to the school to play ball. Greg's team lost almost all its games that summer, but Greg himself batted .285. He almost always called Breanne to tell her where he was going, and he went where he said he was going, except for an occasional unscheduled stop at 7–11 for a quick game of Space Invaders. He was almost afraid to think about the fact that he had friends, that they called him as often as he called them, that he'd had the same friends for months now. At the same time, it seemed like the most natural thing in the world, like the dark-brown hair at the base of his spine that he could barely see in the mirror and that Breanne's fingers touched when she rubbed his back. He didn't rub hers anymore. Once in awhile he saw Maria in the park or at the store and she blushed and said hello and so did he.

The baby kept growing.

Every day Andy sat in his chair, watching the birds and writing. He had nearly filled the stenographer's pad with his tiny, absolutely vertical handwriting, and late one night, in a sudden panic like that of the four-packs-a-day man who runs out of cigarettes after the stores have closed, he prowled the house in search of something else to write in. Finally, in a back corner of Ruth's lingerie drawer – which still smelled softly and sadly and a little sourly of her – he came upon a diary. A bound diary with gold embossed lettering and a gold padlock which wasn't locked, although the ridiculously thin and tiny key was in the box with the book. It was a five-year diary, and the first two years' worth of spaces were neatly written in.

Once he realised what it was, Andy was furious. He'd never known Ruth kept a diary. He wondered suddenly – and was physically sickened by the thought – whether hidden all over this house were other things, fat pink collections of trivial secrets she'd kept from him, not even locked because she'd childishly trusted him or because she'd thought he wouldn't be interested enough to invade her privacy.

She'd been right. With the sharp scissors from her sewing basket, he cut out without reading a word the pages she'd filled in the pink-and-gold diary, crumbled them, and put them in the trash. Then, his fingers clumsy with the key, he locked up the now-blank book, laid it back in its box, and put it on top of his own dresser, in full view, for his own future use. Ruth owed him that.

The process of writing interested him. All his life he'd repeatedly been brought up short by the realisation that other people simply didn't see reality. He was used to seeing eyes glaze and attention wander whenever he tried to talk about the latest evidence on the health hazards of marijuana, the thinning of the ozone layer, the contamination of the city water supply, the coming clash between young and old over the maintenance of the Social Security system. Not that he wanted them to *do* anything, or thought that anyone could. He just wanted them to be aware, and they weren't. After a time, they weren't even interested. He should have let them all go to hell.

Instead, he was writing. The words came out sometimes in streams, sometimes one by one like hard, brown stools. They were the words he'd meant to say in the sense that they were the words he'd formed in his mind and intended to transfer to paper, but, unused to expressing himself in this way, he was never sure that they had much to do with him. He wrote autobiographically, starting with the deaths of his family – an incident which, he acknowledged now, had probably been pivotal in his life, although that acknowledgment was based solely on what he'd read of psychological theory and not on anything personal. He wept when he wrote about that. Now he was writing about his days with the band and he was aware of emotion there, though he called it different things at different times – nostalgia, pride, anger.

Anger. He hadn't wanted to get married in the first place. He hadn't wanted children. Now she was going to have this baby, and something would be wrong with it if that boy was allowed to stay in the house.

And so, every night before he finished his writing and went to bed, Andy wrote something about the boy. A curse, an imprecation, a warning. He had no clear notion yet as to who would ever read what he was writing, but the boy would understand the words.

'You are bad seed. You are bad blood. You do not and cannot belong to anyone. You will destroy anyone you try to love.' And Andy understood the words, too, as if they were about himself.

Near the end of June, the adoption was finalised, an event so anti-climactic and artificial that Breanne found it more annoying than celebrating. Though she tried to play it down ('You're already my son'), she could tell it meant something to Greg. They were waiting in the hallway of the courthouse for Melinda, who was late. They had arranged to meet for breakfast an hour before, in order to go over last-minute details and, Melinda said, to calm everybody down. But Melinda had seemed to be as nervous as anyone, and Breanne worried. What was she afraid of? That the judge would say no? That Breanne would say no? Or – the thought had first occurred to her early this morning and, preposterous as it probably was, she'd been unable to put it out of her mind – that Greg would say no?

She and Greg and Andy had waited almost the whole hour in the orange-and-chrome snackbar in the basement of the courthouse, and Melinda had not come. Now it was fifteen minutes until their scheduled court appearance, and there was still no sign of her. Breanne paced. Greg kept scuffing at the pattern in the gray tile floor. Andy sat upright on the narrow bench, his legs crossed so that his dark socks showed below his magenta-and-navy striped pants, busily writing in a pink-and-gold book that looked to Breanne like a junior high school girl's diary.

He had barely said a word to them all morning, which made her uneasy even though she knew that anything he said would probably not approximate what he meant. He had insisted on coming; she didn't know why, and his attempts to explain had, of course, made no sense ('I am *farmer*,' he had insisted, and, again 'I am *fantasy*'). But Greg hadn't objected, had even seemed pleased.

When she'd asked what he was writing in the diary, he had only shrugged. Her father's handwriting was so cramped and upright that it could hardly be called cursive. She remembered typing his letters to the editor when she was growing up, so irritated by the nearly indecipherable script that she'd barely paid attention to the ideas, though she knew she was supposed to – after all, her mother typed, too. Claire didn't. Later, when Breanne would read his letters in the paper, she'd be shocked by their intelligence and their close, cramped, upright reasoning, and by the fact that they seemed in some confusing way always to miss the point.

One time while she was in college he'd written her a letter. To this day she didn't know why. There had been nothing in it that he hadn't said to her a dozen times before and wouldn't say a dozen times again: The world was going to hell in a handbasket. At that solipsistic point in her life, all her father's opinions had somehow seemed to be directed hurtfully toward her, but even so there was nothing to justify the terror she'd experienced when she'd picked it up from the mailbox in the dormitory basement. *Terror*. As if the letter could harm her. As if her father's anger would get inside her head.

At ten minutes before ten Melinda hurried into sight. The heels of her sandals clicked on the floor and her hair was tousled. 'I'm sorry,' she gasped. 'I had a flat tire. How is everybody?'

'Fine,' said Greg.

'Fine,' said Breanne. 'A little nervous.'

Andy looked up from his writing, looked back down, appeared to finish a sentence, closed and locked the little book, put it into his coat pocket, stood up. He said nothing.

'Melinda,' said Breanne, 'this is my father, Andy Novak. Daddy, this is our social worker.'

'Mr Novak.' Breanne had warned the social worker that her father wanted to come, and Melinda, obviously surprised, had agreed. Now she shook his hand in both of hers in a gesture of welcome and salutation that somehow offended Breanne, as if Melinda were taking the enemy's side, or usurping her place, or missing some important piece of information that would endanger them all. 'I'm glad you could come this morning. It's a real family celebration, isn't it?'

Be careful, thought Breanne, and had to resist an impulse to step between Melinda and her father. Aloud, she said, 'We don't have much time.'

Melinda peered into a pocket mirror and smoothed her hair. 'Let's go on up. It's Courtroom 2, on the second floor.' In the elevator she asked them again, 'How are you all doing?'

'Fine,' said Greg.

Andy smiled politely and said nothing.

Breanne said, 'I'm nervous.'

As the elevator doors whirred open onto the brown vaulted second floor of the courthouse, Melinda touched her shoulder. 'Don't worry. You guys are as ready for this as anybody I've known. It's the third door down on the left.'

But what if the judge says no? Breanne thought desperately. What if Greg says no? What if, as in some awful dream when your body won't do what you tell it to, what if the judge asks me and *I* say no? What if my father does something awful? And she knew she hadn't yet named what was really worrying her.

'Novak,' said the bailiff.

They sat around a rectangular table at the front of the

courtroom. Besides the four of them there were only the bailiff, a short stocky blond man in a gray suit who stood by the door with his hands behind his back; the court recorder, whose dark, quick hands on the eerily silent typewriter seemed the only live thing about her; and the judge, balding, bespectacled, unsmiling, raised on his podium above them all.

The bailiff came forward and read their names: Breanne Susan Novak hereby petitions the court for the adoption of the minor child Gregory Thomas Thurber. The judge silently read through the papers while the rest of them sat there, and Breanne was as distracted by the stillness of the recorder's black hands against her white dress and the blue typewriter as she had been by their swift, purposeful movement a moment ago. The judge took off his glasses and began to ask questions in what at first seemed to Breanne a kindly if essentially indifferent tone.

Yes, Your Honor, said Melinda, she was recommending this adoption. Breanne and Greg had worked through some difficult issues since placement and there was evident bonding taking place.

Yes, Your Honor, Breanne said, she could financially support this child. She was a financial analyst; she told him her salary; he nodded.

Yeah, Greg said, he was doing all right in school. Yeah, he had a lot of friends.

'And you, sir,' said the judge, squinting down at Andy, 'what is your relation to all of this?'

Hastily Melinda started to introduce him, but Andy cut her off. 'I'm *famous*,' he said.

'Famous.' The judge was not amused.

'I am *famished*.'

'He means he's family,' Greg said. Andy glared at him and nodded.

'He's had a stroke,' Breanne said. 'He has expressive aphasia. It's hard for him –'

'Yes,' said the judge.

'He's *minimal*,' said Andy, scowling. 'I *hate* him.'

'He means he loves me,' said Greg.

But the judge had apparently lost interest. He looked down at the decree in front of him and recited: 'Breanne Novak, do you love this child as if he were your own?'

'He *is* my own. Yes.'

'Do you intend to do your best to support him, to attend to his physical and psychological needs, to do all the things that a real parent would do?'

Breanne swallowed and forced herself to say only, 'Yes.'

'Do you understand that he has all the legal rights of a child born to you, that you are responsible for supporting him until he is eighteen or otherwise emancipated, that upon your death he will inherit as if he had been born to you?'

'Yes.'

'Gregory Thurber, do you want this woman to be your mother? Do you love her? Do you accept her? Do you want to stay with her until you grow up and are out on your own?'

'Yes,' Greg said without hesitation, and squeezed Breanne's hand, then added, 'Your Honor.'

The judge pulled the papers to him and signed them with a flourish, reciting the legal formalities and the date. The recorder's fingers flew. Then the judge looked up, smiled for the first time, and said, 'Congratulations.'

In the hall Melinda said, 'That's it! We're through!' She shook their hands. When she offered her hand to Andy he took it, but his eyes were on Greg, who met his gaze. 'Now we all have to go down to the records office for Greg's birth certificate. They'll alter it, Breanne, so that your name and age and place of birth appear on it.'

'That's crazy,' said Breanne. 'He knows he's adopted.'

But Greg, who was used to altering things more permanent than birth certificates, put his arm around her and practically skipped out of the room.

20

'Breanne,' said the voice on the tape. 'A nice, deep, cleansing breath.'

Greg watched Breanne take that kind of breath and found himself doing the same. He was kneeling beside her on the living-room floor, helping her practice. Some lady from work was going to be her actual coach, somebody he'd probably met and didn't remember. They didn't trust him to do it. His mother's head and knees were propped up on pillows, and her stomach rose huge above everything.

'Now, coach,' said the voice of the teacher, and Greg pretended she was talking to him. 'Check your partner's relaxation.'

Gently, as Breanne had shown him, he took her wrist in his hand and lifted it from the floor. Her arm was heavy. He moved it from side to side. He let it go and it thumped onto the floor. They both giggled.

'Now,' said the teacher, 'check her legs.' Greg blushed furiously and slid his hand under Breanne's knees. He could feel them clearly through her jeans. Carefully he lifted, and her knees came up a little way while her heels stayed down. That meant she was relaxed. He smiled.

'Contract your right arm,' the teacher commanded.

'Contract your right arm,' Greg echoed. Breanne raised her right arm a few inches straight in front of her. Greg ran his hands along the muscles of her arm and shoulder and found them tense, the way they were supposed to be, then lifted her other arm and her legs one by one and let them plop satisfyingly to the floor. 'Release your arm,' he said when he was ready, and Breanne's right arm fell.

He knew what she was doing. She was showing him how to do this so he'd feel a part of things. She was trying to give him power so he wouldn't just take it, so he wouldn't hurt the baby. It wouldn't work.

'Contract your left arm,' he commanded on the teacher's cue. 'Contract your left leg. Contract your right arm, your left arm, your right leg.' She did as he told her and most of the time she did it right, so that Greg was proud of her. Proud of them both. It excited him that you could learn such precise control over parts of your body. In bed at night he'd been practicing, too.

Once or twice he had to remind her: 'Relax!' Her face was flushed, her hair wet and curly around her forehead, and he had never felt so close – to her, to the baby, to anyone in his life. She trusted him. 'Relax!' he said again, more tenderly, and her body relaxed into his waiting hands.

21

One Saturday morning in Breanne's eighth month – hot in the city, hotter on the plains, sky an unflinching and glorious blue – she went to the mountains for the day with friends from work and Greg stayed with Andy. She'd been pleasantly surprised that the arrangements had worked out so smoothly, that she'd dared to ask and her son had wanted to go and her father had agreed to keep him; remembering how bad things used to be between them still made her giddy.

It was tempting to believe that the worst was over, that these two difficult and beloved people had found a way to make peace with each other. Breanne knew better. Her father's vulnerability had been, all her life, nearly too much to bear. And now there was her son's vulnerability, how much he could be hurt by forces over which she had no power even though she was, fiercely, his mother. But for today, for this single beautiful midsummer, she was going to leave them alone together, and she was going to believe it would be good for them both.

Already late to meet the others, she just dropped Greg off at the end of her father's driveway. She'd stop in for tea when she picked him up, or bring something back for supper for the three of them. Her feet reaching the pedals only with considerable discomfort, because her stomach bulged against the steering wheel, she made a clumsy U-turn in the gravel road and pulled away. In the rearview mirror she glimpsed her father's pleasant, low-slung, blond-brick house among the rocks and pines, Greg's bright-orange T-shirt a cheery spot of color approaching it.

Suddenly frightened, she knew she would always remember this scene, and she didn't know why: The quiet house, the pretty day, the orange and green and blue and brown. A shiver passed through her and for a moment she was a little dizzy, sensations not unfamiliar to her these last few months. She tried to rest her forehead on the steering wheel until they passed, but couldn't quite reach it.

She took careful note: The liquid singing of the birds, the faint and rapidly fading crunch of Greg's sneakers across the gravel, the fringed shadows of the pines moving in the wind. She could isolate no foreboding detail, nothing skewed. Later, she would believe for a while that what happened between her son and her father that day was somehow her fault, that she had – through ignorance or inattention or a misguided need for peace and escape – missed the one clue that would have saved them all.

As Breanne made the turn off her father's road onto the highway, the baby kicked hard. Breanne caught her breath joyfully and told herself it was going to be a perfect day.

The last time Greg had been alone with Andy, the old man had a stroke, so today Greg was a little nervous. But in a weid way he was kind of looking forward to it. It was sort of a challenge. His mother was always uptight around the old man, and Greg knew some of that had to do with him. He was determined to make friends with Andy if it killed them both.

Shit, he could see why somebody like Andy would feel trapped and cheated, and why he'd act pissed at everybody and everything. Greg himself used to feel like that, and he was just a kid – a pretty mature kid, because of all the crap he'd been through, but still a kid. The difference between him and Andy was that he'd learned. He'd gotten out of it before it was too late. Andy never would.

That made Greg feel sorry for the old man, and gave him a pleasant sense of superiority, out of which he vowed to himself: I'll talk to him, I'll listen to the weird stuff he says and I'll be the only one who can understand what he means, I'll read to him if he wants me to, and I'll sit and watch *Meet the Press* with him, even if it is an incredibly stupid show, and I'll drink his tea, which I can stand if I put enough milk and sugar in it. It won't hurt me to be nice to the guy for one day. After all, he is supposed to be my grandfather.

But it would hurt him, and Greg knew it then, although he would not have been able to identify the knowledge. There was also another strong and unnamed conviction drawing him to Andy: This guy has something to teach me, he has something that I need, whatever its price, in order to grow up sane.

So it was with a buoyant step and a complicated sense of his place in the world that Greg approached his grandfather's house on that sunny summer day. Noticing the dry grass growing up over his shoes, he thought he'd offer to mow. Wondering, somewhat smugly, how much of a mess the house would be in, he decided he could clean it up. Maybe Andy would be pleased.

Andy would never be pleased with him. Greg knew that. A long time ago, when he was first adopted, he'd stayed overnight with Andy, and he'd stolen a retractable measuring tape from the garage. He didn't know why exactly; he hadn't known why then. Because he could get away with it. Because it gave him some weird kind of power in the house of this powerful old man. Because it was neat the way you pushed the red button and the tape went whirring out.

He hadn't really stolen it, because he'd changed his mind and put it back. Well, not *back*, exactly, but he'd sneaked it out of his pocket and put it on the shelf under the kitchen counter. Andy had seen him do it; Greg had meant for him to. He'd wanted him to understand that it was only because he wanted him to be his grandfather that he hadn't kept the tape. But all Andy understood was that Greg had stolen the tape in the first place, and so he would never be pleased with anything Greg ever did.

But today Greg felt like Superman. He could do anything. He could win the old man over. Maybe not to be his grandfather, but at least not to hate him so much. Whistling between his teeth, he rang the doorbell.

During the few minutes it took Andy to answer the door, Greg's mind abruptly filled with images of danger: Sherry's eyes magnified by her tears, the redwood bird-feeder splintering on its post with hundreds of birds inside splitting open, Andy's hard brown eyes popping like bugs you step on in the street.

He rubbed his eyes. He was seeing the eclipse again, clouds tearing away from the hidden moon, clouds and moon bleeding.

He barely had time to realise what he was seeing and to wonder what it meant, when Andy opened the door. A dark figure on a dark background, not saying anything. The blood moon made a funny sound and disappeared; it was morning again, sun so bright Greg could hardly make out the outline of the old man in his house like a cave, not moving toward him at all but somehow making him go inside.

Andy had been waiting for this. He'd seen his chance when Breanne had called and asked him – apologetically, as if she were imposing, which she was – to keep the boy for the day.

He was a bit discomfited when she didn't come in, for he'd strategised carefully how he would handle that. He had envisioned himself behaving perfectly normally, neither too distant nor too pleasant, until she was safely out of the way, and he had rather admired in himself the skill and self-discipline that would require. He would have got nowhere in his life without, especially, self-discipline.

He resented his daughter's bad manners, her eagerness to get away to the mountains with friends and leave him with the responsibility for this boy. The boy, of course, wasn't her son and never would be, wasn't his grandson, wasn't flesh and blood. She had taken him in out of a misguided, soft-headed desire to do good and by now, Andy could see, had actually taken a liking to him.

Andy didn't understand that at all, and it angered him.

His love for his daughter had always, from the day of her birth, been so laced with anger that the two responses were virtually indistinguishable from each other.

All her life, Breanne had gone out of her way to hurt him and her mother, to do things they could not be expected to understand or accept.

When she was in high school he had given her the money to buy a National Honor Society pin, which she had said she didn't especially want but which he wanted, her mother wanted. As far as he knew she had never bought it, and she had never, to this day, repaid him the ten dollars.

Then one morning when she was a sophomore in college he had gone to work before seven and had seen her walking up the hill toward her dorm arm-in-arm with her boyfriend for all the world to see, for the people he supervised at the store to see and know right away what was going on, his own daughter. She told him she had had a breakfast date, but she didn't even try to keep a straight face. For three months after that, although he continued to pick up and deliver her laundry as scheduled every Friday over her protests, he had not spoken to her.

And now, this boy. She expected too much. But this he could do something about. He let the boy in.

'Hi, Andy.'

The boy didn't call him Grandpa. That angered Andy, though he would have protested if he had. 'Do you wallow some talcum?' he demanded.

'Sure,' said the boy, walking right past him and not bothering to translate.

When Andy went to put the water on for tea, he thought the kitchen smelled vaguely of gas. Early this morning – he'd just gotten up; everyone was a bit groggy first thing in the morning – he had turned the burner on and forgotten to light it, and the odor had been nearly overpowering. He loathed himself when he did old-man things like that. Boys like this one laughed, and they had reason to.

That had happened hours ago and there was no imminent danger now. But the memory of danger in the close air of his kitchen excited and distressed him, gave him a headache. He shook his head irritably and tried to strike a match.

'Hey,' said the boy behind him. Andy jumped and dropped the match. It fell inside the burner, where it lit with a small blue pop. 'I could mow your lawn while I'm here. Give me something to do.'

'That won't be nasty,' Andy growled.

The boy tried unsuccessfully to suppress a guffaw. 'You mean *necessary*,' he said insolently. Andy scowled and nodded.

The water in the kettle, still warm from his last pot of tea, was already chugging to the boil. For a moment Andy nearly forgot the presence of the boy for the presence of the agitated molecules of water and the corresponding agitated pain in his own head.

'Want me to clean your house? Straighten it up or something? It's sort of a mess.'

'The house is furious,' Andy said firmly. 'Fancy. Fine.' By now he was never sure when he had actually said the right word, among all the others of equal weight and resonance that crowded his head and burst out of his mouth. He dropped a teabag into a mug, thinking bitterly of Ruth as he always did whenever he performed a domestic chore. He poured steaming water over it, worrying about spilling any in front of the boy. 'Shoe and mono?'

'Sure,' said the boy, and Andy marveled again at how readily they understood each other. The boy took a step toward the refrigerator to get the milk.

'*Yes!*' Andy snapped, and the boy glared at him, shrugged, and stayed where he was.

They drank their tea together in the bright, dusty living room. The boy squirmed in his chair. Andy's headache had coalesced into a beam of pain like a searchlight between his eyes.

'So how've you been?' asked the boy.

Andy made no reply, of course. He heard birds overhead, on their way somewhere; Ruth would have been hurrying to the window with the binoculars. The house was quiet.

'I'm doing pretty good in school,' the boy offered.

'Wick. Warm. Way.'

The boy stared at him, uncomprehending this time, and Andy saw that there was no point trying to correct his grammar. The public schools in this country did nothing but waste taxpayers' money. It was disgraceful.

The boy was squinting at the television screen now as if he could will it to life, and coldly Andy wondered if perhaps he could, the power wasted on ridiculous situation comedies and violence-ridden police shows that would eventually render him incapable of distinguishing fantasy from reality. That, in Andy's opinion, was the trouble with young people today; they had no firm grasp on what was real.

'How's the tray?' he inquired, biding his time.

'Fine,' said the boy, but Andy could tell from the strained expression on his face that he didn't like tea, he was being polite. Andy was glad he had no soda pop or juice to offer; it pleased him to think of the tea, both bitter and sickly sweet in the boy's mouth.

'I don't see how we're ever going to get out of this marble we're in,' Andy said flatly.

'The world's a mess,' the boy agreed.

Abruptly, Andy was aware of how hard Greg was trying, how precipitously close the two of them were to loving each other, how much they could be said to need each other. Breanne would say they needed each other. He did not dare allow such a thing to happen. He reminded himself that this boy was dangerous in a way only he could appreciate. The boy was an anomaly, an aberration, so filled with evil that there were times when Andy did not think of him as human. At the same time, he was a teenage boy like all the rest. Like the ones who kept knocking his mailbox down. Like the ones who laughed at him when he said the wrong word, or would if they knew. Andy had never had much use for teenagers, even when he was one himself a long time ago.

'There will be a newberry walnut in the next disease,' Andy stated deliberately. To his own ears, the foolishness of the words made the threat more sinister, and in the boy's young face he saw both amusement and fear.

'I ain't afraid of nuclear war,' the boy said sullenly.

Andy raised his eyebrows. 'Ate? Able? There's no such word as ache.'

The boy said nothing. Seeing that he was trying to control his temper, Andy said to himself that that would be harder today than the boy had ever imagined.

'You should be afraid,' Andy went on as planned. 'If there is a noodle window, all hungrys will die.'

'The human race ain't worth shit anyway.'

Andy flinched at the boy's persistence in using that word, and furiously asked himself again what in the world our educational system was teaching these days. He himself had always done exceptionally well in school, and despite his background he had never been a problem to society in any way. People were entirely too willing these days to make excuses for criminals and welfare cheats and this clever, dangerous boy.

'The track with you *kelp*,' Andy said, curling his lip on the word as disgustedly as if it were the one he had meant to say, 'is that you do not understand the real worm. All you care about is verry-o grammar and that goddamn music.'

'The trouble with you *old people*,' the boy shot back with equal malice, 'is you don't know *nothin*'. You've lived all these years, and what for? You –'

'Shut up.'

Andy had seen what he was waiting for. The anger. He had known it was there; rage like that could not be controlled forever. His own anger rumbled inside him like an idling beast, and the wounds where it had fed on him over the years were fiery hot. He got to his feet and stood over the boy.

'Shut up!' he cried. His voice rang in the empty house. 'Shut *up*!'

'Make me.'

The boy stood up, too. He was almost as tall as Andy, almost as enraged. Andy's headache seemed to have grown

145

wings and talons, and was ready to tear off the top of his head.

Now. Now was the time.

The old man was never going to love him. It was stupid to keep on trying.

But maybe if he acted right.

No matter how hard his mother pretended, the old man was never going to be his grandfather.

But maybe if he learned the right code words.

The old man knew the truth about him, knew a truth that Greg didn't even know about himself.

Knew he wasn't safe to be in a family.

Knew he wasn't fit to be loved. Others had known, too, and had tried to show him. The man with the rubber band and the cigarettes. The woman with the belt. Sherry, who had had to die to get away from him. His real mother and his real father, who had just given him away because they couldn't stand him, they hated him, they were afraid of him.

Breanne didn't know yet.

His mother didn't know the truth about him, and he couldn't let her find out or she would leave him, too.

They were right to be afraid of him. This old man who wasn't his grandfather had better be afraid of him, too.

Andy went into his bedroom and removed the pink-and-gold diary from its box on his dresser. His hand hesitated above the stenographer's notebook but he drew it back, appalled by his driving impulse to let the boy know all he had written, all he had put into words about his own life. He wanted Greg to know him. Even, he realised, to like him. To *love* him – and Andy recognised this as part of this boy's life-threatening power, which was greater than even he had imagined.

He carried the diary in both hands back to the living room. The boy was sitting like a child, with one foot tucked up under him, staring out at the empty birdfeeder. When Andy stopped in front of him, he did not look up.

One by one Andy turned the pages of the diary. It took him long minutes to locate the right place. The springs of the boy's chair made tiny squeaks as he breathed and shifted his weight. He was looking at Andy's hands now, at the pages of the diary flickering.

'Here,' said Andy at last, and handed it over. The boy did not take it, even raised his hands to shove it away. Having anticipated something like this, Andy placed the book on the boy's thigh. His finger marking the page grazed the boy's protesting hand, and they both winced.

'Rally,' Andy ordered.

The boy looked at him as if he did not understand, and the lie infuriated him.

'Rabbit. Roast. Redman,' he said before he could stop himself. The boy's lips moved almost silently to help Andy state the command accurately: '*Read!*' This boy, above all others, always knew what he meant.

Finally the boy accepted the book, as Andy had known he would, and bent his head over it. Sunlight like a knife blade struck across the back of his neck. Andy sat down in his chair, with Ruth's hard, cylindrical pillow positioned behind his neck, eyes closed, his head throbbing, his fists in his lap, and visualised the words he had written there in the diary. It was as though he were speaking them aloud, with a fluency he'd never had in his life, even before the stroke.

'You are bad seed. You are bad blood. You do not and cannot belong to anyone. You destroy anyone you try to love.

'Get away from my daughter. She is a stranger to you. She is not your mother. You do not have a mother and you never will.'

The words in the old man's tiny, straight-up-and-down, hard-to-read handwriting were suddenly swimming in red. Greg shook his head violently. The old man's rage hit him like hail, hard chunks of ice that could put his eye out, or his heart.

'Think about it,' the old man instructed him in the

written words like blood-red bugs. 'Your sister is dead. Your mother left you and you will never see her again. Nobody knows who your father is, and you will never know.

'Think about it. They are all gone. They did everything they could to get rid of you. They beat you and they burned you and they left you alone.

'*Think about it.* You are evil and you are alone and you will destroy everybody who tries to love you. You will always be alone.'

Something was happening. Greg felt something hot, a blood-hot cloud, seeping through him from his toes to the top of his head.

'You are not like other people. You know that. You are different. The older you get the more different you will become. You are a monster. You have a monstrous power. You know that.'

Greg knew that. He saw things: Sherry's face. Heard things: Voices wailing, voices calling his name, voices so far away he could hardly make them out, and still going away from him. Felt things: Tight fingers around his balls and an ache tightening around his chest, like a wide belt. If he looked in a mirror he would see what he'd always guessed was there: Something bad, something alien, looking back at him.

'My daughter is going to have her own child, a real child, her own flesh and blood. Then she won't want you. Think about it.

'*Think about it, boy.*'

Greg did think about it, and what he thought was no surprise. The old man was right. Breanne had tricked him. The social worker, of course, had tricked him. Worst, he had tricked himself. The old man was his mortal enemy and his only true friend. In a weird way, the old man *was* his grandfather, related to him by blood.

'Leave.'

Greg looked up sharply. What was the old man saying? Leave? Live? Love? His vision was blurred by tears and his hearing by a ringing in his ears. And for a terrible minute there were lots of Andys in the world, lots of cracked old voices telling him exactly what to do.

Andy said the word again. 'Leave. Live. Love.' Holding a fresh, steaming cup of tea, he sat now with his back to the bright window, and the framed blue sky behind him threw his face into shadow.

Now – right before his eyes, obscuring everything else, more real than anything else, made up of everything else – Greg saw:

feathers flying. Blood from the opened neck of a chicken hung upside down from the clothesline in Mrs Decker's farmyard. The other kids didn't notice or scampered away; Greg, fascinated and crying, stayed to watch until all the blood was drained away and the chicken stopped jerking.

People coming at him with the rubber band, the belt, the little red-glowing cigarette. Coming at him to hurt him with things he couldn't see, things he had to find a use for. His door splintering, his hand splintering, his heart splintering into bright-red shards that embedded themselves everywhere, worked themselves into his bloodstream and his breath.

Sherry's eyes. Loving him. Hating him. Blowing up.

Blowing up. Andy blowing up. Andy in flames. Andy in terrible pain. Greg yelled. Andy and all the mean things that lived inside him, that lived inside Greg, all the things that had made him so mad for his whole life exploding, dying, slamming down on the world like the fiery hail after a bomb.

He could make that happen.

When he made that happen, he would die, too. He would blow up, and he would hurt everybody who had ever hurt him, and he would hurt Breanne before she could hurt him, and then it would all be over.

'Leave. Live. Love.' Andy was stuck on the sequence of nonsense words that made perfect sense to Greg. 'Leave. Live. Love. Leave. Live. Love.'

'You *monster*!'

The diary flew out of Greg's hands and hit the old man

in the face. Greg saw blood. He leaped to his feet. The lamp on the table between their two chairs toppled, glass broke, but the noise didn't go on for very long. Andy groaned and put his hands to his temples.

'You monster! I'll kill you! I'll kill you all!' Greg stumbled out of the house.

His head boomed, as if it would explode, too. He hoped it would.

He ran into the pine woods behind Andy's house, but he didn't run far, not nearly far enough to be safe. A branch slapped his cheek, drew tears and blood. His ankle turned, something cracked, and pain shot up his shin.

He flung himself down on his hands and knees under a thin tree and forced himself to look back. Back. At his mother's womb. At Sherry's eyes. At his other mother's arms.

At the old man's house, now a ball of fire.

22

He watched her. He watched the baby.

The hard brown eyes of the dead old man crawled out from under the city streets like cockroaches, too fast to catch, too hard to squash even if you stomped your heel right onto the shell. They followed Greg. They raced inside him.

He'd killed Andy. Sometimes – watching his mother move inside their house, wanting to go to her, wanting to squash her stomach back into the right shape – he told himself he hadn't meant to. But he had. He'd thought about the old man exploding with his anger, and it had happened just that way.

Greg had missed the memorial service. He wouldn't have gone anyway. He'd watched his mother getting ready, seen her stricken face, heard her call his name as she called over and over and he never answered, never would answer. He'd heard her tell somebody her father was going to be cremated. That struck Greg as so funny that he had to hide his face in his arm to stifle the laughter.

Until he realised that the old man's smoke and ashes would seep into everything, that he'd be breathing the old man in. Then he ran behind the garage and threw up, trying to keep it quiet. His mother drove right past him and didn't see him. She was gone a long time. He thought she might never come back.

But she did. And he watched her. And he watched the baby.

23

Breanne started across another intersection, obeying the traffic signals as if they had some meaning this late at night, served some purpose. The streets were deserted. She hadn't seen a vehicle or another pedestrian since she'd stepped off the almost-empty bus some blocks back.

High on the walls of the bus, creased a little where they had for so long followed the curve to the ceiling, had been posters of missing children. 'Have You Seen Me?' The same few faces on every bus she rode, until she began to think she might have seen the actual children somewhere, maybe somehow did know something about their disappearance.

The same few missing faces, and on some of them the 'Date Missing' a decade or more ago. She couldn't imagine – and it made her inexplicably furious – of what use a blurred photo of a four-year-old could be in finding someone who was now fourteen. By now the pictures had become symbolic in her mind, representing every child who had ever been lost.

But Greg, her own missing child, wasn't up there. Exhausted, desperate, she'd kept searching for his face.

The amber street lights threw everything into an odd bas-relief. Buildings, marquees, planters, café railings, trash – all became subtly different from what Breanne knew them to be. Unable to see her footing past her swollen belly, she stumbled a little, and put out her hands into thin air.

The white 'Walk' lights had, of course, lit up on all four corners at once, programmed to stop all traffic and allow pedestrians – briefly – to scurry in any direction. The signal lured her, over the very slight bump where 19th and Tremont Streets met. She felt vulnerable and guilty out there, crossing diagonally, even though she did this several times every workday, even though the lights and the crosswalk clearly gave permission, even though there was no traffic anyway. She kept glancing up at the light pole and down at the painted lines on the pavement to make sure she was right, she hadn't misperceived or been tricked. Of course, the light did change before she reached the other curb. Advanced pregnancy made her slow; fatigue and worry made her slightly unstable on her feet. Now the light flashed red, angry and erratic, warning her, 'Don't Walk.' But she was already exposed in the middle of the intersection; she had no choice but to walk. She tried to hurry, but for a few confusing moments she wasn't sure she was moving at all.

Just before she was ready to step up onto the curb, she knew someone was watching her. A crazed, lost kid, she thought, both older and younger than his years. Terrified, fighting for his life, *dangerous*. Cumbersomely, she whirled. The weight of her body and the protrusion of her briefcase threw her slightly off balance. She clutched at the air for support, found none, but miraculously did not fall.

Greg wasn't there. No one was there. But he was watching her, and she and her baby were in danger.

The street lights were vaguely the color of her flesh. They made her flesh look sallow, pocked. They reflected in bizarre ripples and whorls from the steel-and-glass towers. Here and there a string of blue-white corridor lights cut across a building like a choker, like a slash across a long throat, as cleaning crews moved from one floor to the next. Her own office building was in the next block, not among the tallest and so still hidden from her view. It seemed to her that she'd been trying to get to it for a long time.

Against the murky sky she couldn't really make out the

outlines of the buildings. But she could feel the way the structures tunneled and sheared the air, hear the slight distortions they made in the sounds of the city and the smaller sounds of those trapped within it. She knew the baby could feel and hear those things, too, could absorb her fear. So could Greg. They were all trapped together.

She did not believe Greg was dead. She did not believe he was lost to her forever. She could barely believe her father was dead, though she and Claire had scattered his ashes like magic dust. She would never see him again, but his love like anger was more than alive.

Breanne was afraid. Afraid for both her children, either of whom might well destroy the other. Afraid for herself, a dimensionless fear. And sad. So sad that the grief bunched and kicked, her abdomen cramped violently, and for a few moments she was doubled over with pain and unable to move in the dangerous nighttime city.

She wanted *Daddy*. The Daddy he hadn't been for a long time, had never been and had always been. The wanting was primal, and for a while – an instant, a lifetime – she was lost to it, it was all she was.

She hadn't been able to stay at home tonight. The house had been acutely lonely, and teeming with presences. She was afraid of Greg. Admitting that had brought swift retributive grief, and she'd cried out, but it was true: She was afraid of her son. Her father's love for her had always felt like anger; hers for her son now felt like fear.

She wanted him to come home. She wanted him to stay away. It was his home, too, and eventually he would come there for her.

So she had come to work. It wasn't unusual for analysts to work late and odd hours. Many of them had little to keep them at home – like Breanne herself before Greg, until the baby – and accessing the mainframe was easier at other than peak usage times. She hoped somebody else would be working tonight.

She hurried. Her feet ached, and the spot between her shoulders that always hurt from carrying her briefcase glowed with concentrated pain like a red-hot dime. The three-block walk from the bus stop to the office seemed impossibly long and arduous tonight. She should have driven. Almost every meter she passed marked an empty space and had its flag up.

She looked up at the buildings and the sky melding together, down at the pink-bathed sidewalk and street and curb with no clear demarcations from one to the other, and suddenly she had no idea where she was.

Panic rose in her like sickness, and for a giddy moment she imagined that the baby would come like that when it was time, through her mouth. She could see the white-on-green street sign telling her she was at the corner of 19th and California Streets; she knew the names of many of the buildings and shops around her. But she did not know where she was. She was lost in a city gone alien. She was alone, and not alone. Greg was somewhere nearby, maybe behind that bending signpost, in the shadowy entrance of that bank, under the bus bench that she seemed to be passing again and again. He was lost. He needed her desperately. He hated her and the baby. He would destroy them both if he could. And he could.

Hearing herself cry out, Breanne pressed a fist against her mouth, as though the sound of her own anguish would put her in greater danger, The briefcase bruised her thigh. Laying one palm against a wall, she blindly turned a corner.

A figure flew at her, scratched her face, tore at her clothes, pulled her tangled hair. She screamed. She tried to jump aside and couldn't. Her groin and belly throbbed, and the baby twisted inside. She thought there was blood on her cheek.

She had walked into a section of metal fencing that had come loose from its stake. It had caught her cuff, popped the button, and ripped the sleeve almost to the elbow. Something had scraped her face, and the wound was beginning to sting. She could barely catch her breath, and she was sweating profusely.

At her feet gaped an enormous hole, perhaps two stories deep. Its bottom and uneven sides were littered with objects she couldn't quite see in the salmon-colored gloom.

Suddenly it seemed vital for her to know exactly what they were, and she realised she would never know – they would forever blow or burrow just out of her reach, or they would fall apart at her touch into unidentifiable pieces, or the unreliable light would alter them from one thing to another to another the longer she stared.

For a moment she had the heady fantasy that the ground would give way and she would slide down into that hole that had been dug, she supposed, for a foundation. That she would have her baby down there, and both of them would die of blood loss and exposure before anyone but Greg even knew they were gone.

The air was heavy and humming. Breanne, like a child, stuck her fingers through the mesh. An amber-tinted cloud had spread among the buildings, so that against it they looked like teeth against a jaundiced tongue. When she caught a glimpse of a star, she was inordinately pleased, relieved. But then she saw that the star was moving along the strip of sky that paralleled the street, and she realised it was a plane at the same instant that its light disappeared.

Against the upright part of the fence, a hot-dog-and-nacho stand hunkered, closed up for the night. Its abandonment disturbed her; somehow she'd assumed that vendors took their carts safely home with them at night. The striped umbrella was folded, like wings; the red doors were shut, and one handle was padlocked to a fence post.

She inched her way along the fence like a zoo animal, made a wary half-circle around the cart – and saw Greg.

Crouching on the dirty pavement partway under the cart. Hands around his knees. Staring at her, reflecting the murky light of the nighttime city and magnifying it a thousand-fold so that his eyes gleamed. Saying nothing, making no sound at all.

She caught her breath and drew back, then said his name and reached out to him, awkwardly sinking to her knees and supporting her weight and her baby's by pressing her palms against the smooth painted side of the cart. She could smell the old paint, the residual odors of grease and meat. Her stomach churned.

It wasn't Greg. It wasn't anybody. It was only the shadows of the cart and the umbrella, distorted by the broken fence, and two crumpled foil bags where his eyes had been.

In the five days and nights since he'd disappeared – since the fire, since her father had died – it had constantly been like this. She'd seen him everywhere, heard his voice and his silences, but when she approached he was never there. Each time she thought she'd found him – or he had found her – she was infused with terror for her baby; each time she lost him again, terror for him took hold.

Painfully she crawled to her feet. For a long moment she stood with head bowed and hands loosely at her swollen sides, fighting for balance. When she thought she wouldn't fall, she risked raising her eyes.

There, just across the street, not twenty yards away, was her office building. The brown brick surface, rectangular shape, arced sign on the window were just clear enough for her to be sure. She nearly called out in relief. She wasn't lost anymore.

A construction bridge spanned the street. Jackhammers had been at work there for months, their ratcheting able to pierce even the sealed windows of the office. The absence of their concentrated noise had contributed to her disorientation tonight. Realising that calmed her.

Though there was no traffic and she could safely have jaywalked, she dared take no chances. She stepped off the solid curb onto the wooden floor of the bridge, which teetered slightly under her weight. The pinkish glow of the street light made confusing stripes of shadow between the slats on the right side. The left wall was pocked with graffiti. Because she couldn't make out most of the words, they came to seem like a secret code, like hex symbols, and she looked away.

She put out her hands and found the rough wooden walls scant inches away on both sides, like the sides of a crate. A high-pitched metallic hum that she hadn't noticed before now climbed rapidly in the confined space of the tunnel until it hurt her ears. She forced herself to keep walking, keep walking, turning a sharp corner, because the path of the tunnel forced her to – and came out the other end onto the little plaza that fronted her building like a yoke.

Abruptly, everything was familiar again. The pattern of the paving stones was the one she admired every day from her window on the eleventh floor and walked across every morning, lunch hour, and evening. The building itself promised shelter and she hurried toward it.

The humming came, of course, from the sculpture on the southeast corner of the plaza. Breanne remembered when they'd put it in. A dozen thin stainless-steel cylinders, from waist-height to well over ten feet tall, constructed and arranged to vibrate at the slightest breeze. Impulsively, she veered to stand inside it.

One lovely Indian summer Saturday last year, she and Greg had come down here for lunch and a noontime concert on the plaza by a local jazz band. She worried that there'd be no Indian summer this year, reminded herself that she wouldn'd knonw until it happened, that an Indian summer was, by definition, a sweet surprise. She remembered how everything had gleamed: the cerulean sky, the black-and-silver buildings and the black-and-gray plaza tiles, the windows and flanks of cars and buses and delivery trucks, the buckles and braid and instruments of the band.

Greg had been *happy*. She remembered, and it saddened her to remember. She had been happy. It was tempting now to dismiss those moments of happiness as unreal or manipulative or insignificant, in the light of all that had happened since and all that was still to happen. Breanne forced herself to remember fully how that day had been. The band had incorporated the singing of the sculpture into its music, had improvised with it. Greg had sat close, had let her put her arm around him.

He'd *played*. He'd used the plaza paving stones as a giant hopscotch court, hopping on one foot and then the other, giggling and hooting like a little boy. He'd played hide-and-seek in the sculpture, peek-a-boo like a baby.

He'd stood among the cylinders like Hansel in the forest, and she'd counted his reflections in the curved polished surfaces, and they'd laughed together, and she hadn't been in the least afraid.

Though now she suspected that she should have been, and that Greg had been terrified.

Grateful for the memory, sustained by it, Breanne ran her hands up and down the cylinders, stopping or altering their motion and sound. Then she slipped free and went in the front door of her building, which welcomed her.

24

There was pale light in the lobby, which served more to create shadows than to illuminate. The floor tiles and the walls were shiny brown. Along the far wall, elevators stood ready, doors silently open to expose brightly lit interiors. It was a long time since Breanne had worked at night; everything looked intensely familiar, under a patina of alienness.

There were the same odors, too, of floor polish and cigarette smoke and, she supposed, of the people who'd left at five or six o'clock and would be coming back in the morning. The sense of trepidation and adventure at entering a deserted building at night was the same, the absurd thrill, as if it gave her some secret knowledge. Her heels were so loud on the tiles that she hesitated after the first few steps to let the clatter and the echoes die down, then hurried to the nearest elevator as fast as she could so that her footsteps came all in a rush.

She punched '11' and the elevator door swept shut. As the car rose, she looked at herself in the mirrored back wall, amazed as usual by the enormity of her belly, by how much space a child could claim even before it was born.

As she got off her elevator, the cleaning crew was just getting on theirs, two women and two men with buckets and brooms, pushing a laden cart. She said, 'Hello,' and was prepared to explain what she was doing here so late, but they paid no attention to her. Their laughter and the music from the gigantic radio nestled among the cleaning supplies on the top of the cart made a little island of sound, like the island of light made by their elevator car until the doors slid shut between them and her.

They had, of course, shut off the corridor lights. It was easier to find her office suite in the dark – the second set of doors on the right past the elevators – than to grope for the light switch. She set her briefcase down and used both hands to fit her key into the lock. It turned easily and the door edged open. Breanne reached around the jamb to turn on the office lights, thus creating her own island in the midst of the dark building, but one she could only imagine because she was in it.

She brought the briefcase in, shut the door, put her keyring back into her purse, and made her way across the reception area to her office cubicle at the back. On her way past the receptionist's desk, she automatically checked her box for messages. Of course there were none; she'd been in all day, and nobody knew she was here tonight.

She had settled herself cumbersomely at her desk, turned on the terminal and the monitor, and spread out her paperwork, when she heard a noise. She looked up. All she saw were the familiar blue-gray walls of her cubicle, the gray filing cabinet, the spider plant happily sending out shoots under the fluorescent lights, the open door. The individual cubicle door did not lock, but, crazily, she cursed herself anyway for having left it open. She kept the papers still, turned off the faint buzzing of the monitor, and listened hard. The silence seemed alive, or made by something alive – a spider, or a web.

The noise came again, and she realised it was a series of noises, from the reception area just outside her door. Two clicks: The opening and closing of the outer door to the suite. Creaking: Footsteps rapidly approaching, but only a few and then they stopped. Then the thick silence again, the building sealed so that no sounds from the city filtered in and no sounds from the occupants, however desperate, could seep out.

Heavily, Breanne stood up. Pain shot upward between her legs, to the base of her spine, into the pit of her stomach, across her ribs and sternum, into her throat. She cried out and clutched at the edge of the desk. When the pain subsided enough for her to stand straight and open her eyes again, her son was crouching in the doorway, bent forward and gasping as though over his own pain.

'Greg!'

He was coming toward her. She was afraid of him. She wanted to take him in her arms, to welcome him home, to prove to him once and for all that he was safe.

'Greg, sweetheart, I won't hurt you. The baby won't hurt you.' She was crooning as if to a maddened animal or a tiny, terrified child. But she was afraid of him.

He'd been crying. His eyes were red, the soft flesh around them puffy. His breath still came hard, as if it hurt. A long, angry scratch that looked to be still bleeding raked the side of his neck. She longed to kiss his eyes, to clean away the dirt and blood from his wound, to start the healing. She knew how. But she was afraid to get that close to him, with the baby between them.

'Where have you been?' she demanded, managing a bit of maternal indignation. 'I've been worried sick about you.'

He reached out to her, hands like rakes, trembling, tines bent. Hands like forceps. Instincts warred in her. She pulled away, though it nearly broke her heart to have to do so. She retreated, keeping the sharp corners and edges of the desk solidly between them.

Her waters broke. The insides of her thighs were suddenly wet and warm and her thin skirt was sticking to her legs.

She gasped. 'The baby!'

For long moments she and Greg stared at each other in utter, shared helplessness. The building was absolutely quiet. The fluorescent lights tinged everything with a faint buzzing, a faint bluish veneer which, she thought wildly, could be peeled off with a fingernail to expose whatever lay underneath.

Amniotic fluid was trickling, gushing down her legs. She struggled to bring her thought processes back under control, to decide what to do. 'Greg,' she said as firmly as she could. 'The baby's coming. It's early. We've got to get to the hospital.'

She started for the door, planning furiously. Cabs sat all night in the hotel taxi stand across the plaza; that would be quicker than calling an ambulance, and much cheaper. Her pelvis contracted, her vaginal walls rippling with pain. She cried out and groped for the doorjamb.

Greg lunged. From his mouth came fetid breath, and a harsh mewling sound like the yowl of a frightened cat. In the split second before he touched her, she felt a hot, hard pressure, and she thought the waters stopped flowing for a moment, the baby stopped moving. Before she could twist out of his reach, Greg's hands were at her sides, fingertips digging in as though to trap the baby, to strangle it, to stop it from being born.

The muscles in her pelvis contracted again. Something seemed to be nudging its way out between her legs, though she didn't think it could be happening so soon. Greg pushed her hard against the stippled wall behind her. She grabbed his wrists and couldn't stop herself from sliding down the wall, pulling him with her until they were both kneeling on the rough, nearly napless, blue-green office carpet that was now spotted and wet.

'Let me go! The baby! I have to get to the hospital!'

But Greg was holding her down. She could not push him away or break his grip. Her energy seemed to be focusing without her will on the baby, the birth of the baby, the tearing of her vaginal wall, the tightening and loosening of muscles deep inside her. Greg had butted his head into her chest like a battering ram; her breasts ached from the force of it. Suddenly, as she tried to relax into the wave of another fierce contraction, she made out the word he was shrieking: 'Mama! Mama!'

25

Hungry cold alone he was going to be left alone again he knew the word now *abandon* she was going to abandon him he would die he would starve and nobody would come except to hurt him to punish him to make him think they loved him so they could leave him she was going to leave him another mother was going to abandon him she was going to have a baby of her own a baby he'd die if she left him alone she was his mother he *needed* her he couldn't take care of himself.

Greg lay beside his mother. His body was partway over hers. In places they looked like one body, felt like one body. His feet and shoulders were wedged back against the cubicle door, holding it shut. His arms were around her neck. His face was against hers. They were both crying.

He didn't dare let her out. He didn't dare let the baby out. If he let either one of them out, he'd be alone forever and then he'd die.

She was groaning. The baby was hurting her, trying to get out. Greg almost thought he remembered that, hurting his mother, trying to be born. He was sorry. She was stroking his hair. He liked that. She was talking to him in a voice so soothing that he listened, thought he knew better, though he listened more to the tone than to the words. He'd been listening to her for hours, he thought, for a long time.

'Greg, let me up. Let me call an ambulance or call a cab. We have to get to the hospital. You come with me. The baby's going to be born. It's coming early. The contractions are only a few minutes apart now.'

No! he thought wildly, and she writhed against the floor though he hadn't moved his body or even thought bad things. *No!*

Now she was breathing the way they'd practiced together, puffing like a little kid's choo-choo train, and he found himself breathing that way, too, as if he were the one having the baby, as if he were helping her.

There was a lot of blood. That scared him, fascinated him, made him sick. When he tried to imagine where inside her that blood was coming from, he couldn't, though he thought he remembered. They were all floating in his mother's blood, the whole world was floating in his mother's blood, the river of blood that would bring the baby out. The whole world was floating in him, in the noise he heard himself making, the noise he knew he'd been making all his life whether anybody else had heard it or not. A wail, like wind when there wasn't any wind, like the crying of a scared monster underneath his bed. He was calling her, and he knew she heard. 'Mama! Maaamaaa!'

She tried to get away from him. He pinned her down. He was stronger than she was. That scared him, infuriated him. He hid his face between her breasts, lifted his knees against her huge stomach.

'Greg. Baby. It's all right. I love you.'

Baby baby baby he had wet himself he had messed himself it was all right his mama would take care of him *no! no!* she would leave him abandon him the baby would make her abandon him she wouldn't want him anymore he would die.

Suddenly she screamed and arched up under him, flinging him off. He could see her belly, her knees drawn up, her cloths scathered where she'd pulled them off, her fists against his chest trying to push him away. He could feel her fists hitting him. '*No!*' he shouted out loud, but she was already on her feet standing over him tugging at the door pushing him out of the way he rolled over so that his cheek was against the rough carpet she stepped over

165

him he got wet he heard her running away from him he would die he would die.

He made himself sit up. He made his mind fill up with pictures of his mother exploding, the baby exploding, blood everywhere, blood all over him, his own blood, too. He heard her yell. Her voice sounded so different from out in the hall that at first he wasn't sure who it was. But he knew she was the one yelling, something was hurting her, and he had caused it. The carpet was wet under him. He ran his hands across the wet places and then raised his fingers to his mouth.

The pictures in his mind, his mother's voice, the smell and taste of the blood and water from inside his mother's body, made Greg strong. He could still stop her. He could stop the baby.

He got to his feet. He crept out of the office, through the bright reception area where the lights hurt his eyes, into the long, dim hallway. He was stalking his mother. He was stalking the baby. He would get them both.

26

Breanne took the hall that led to the right out of the office door, instead of retreating the way she had come. The straight stretch before the corner was longer this way; she felt acutely exposed, and tried to hurry. This route to the elevator required many more steps, and she had no steps to waste, but frantically she hoped it would throw Greg off, confuse him long enough for the elevator to rescue her.

She tried to move soundlessly along the dim hallway, trailing one hand on the cool wall to keep her bearings, to stop herself from falling. Her body throbbed and flared with insistent pain, as though someone who knew her well was hurting her from the inside. Her body was so heavy that she could scarcely guide it, could not predict where the next step would take her, what obstacle she would run into with every step, every gesture, every breath, every thought.

She thought agonisingly, *Greg*, and then struggled to purge from her mind the terrible worry and grief for him. There was the distinct sensation of something pushing back. She turned away from it, took a deep breath, turned the corner of the corridor into another long, straight stretch.

Her baby was being born. This desperate instant was part of the long moment of birth. She was sure she could actually feel the crown of the head protruding – soft, the skull not yet safely closed – and foolishly she tried for a few steps to run with her legs wide apart so that the baby wouldn't be trapped, the eggshell skull wouldn't be crushed. Her own head was aching fiercely; red and black pulsed before her eyes, half-blinding her, and her temples throbbed as if something pounded and clawed to get out or in.

Another contraction brought her straining to her toes, pressed her sweating cheek against the wall, wrenched a cry from her that echoed around the rectangle of the corridor that ringed the building. The astonishingly intimate pressure at her pelvis intensified, blood and birth water spurted, but as far as she could tell the baby didn't move. A new terror enveloped her: The baby born dead, the baby unborn altogether, the baby disintegrating and exploding inside the birth canal, the baby trapped forever by a force of some kind that had entered through the soft top of its head.

Greg, she thought unwillingly, and then was shrieking it aloud. 'Greg! Greg! No!' The hallway served to twist and elongate her words. She had the fantasy that, to someone on the other side of the building, her cry would be trapped and stretched almost beyond recognition. But Greg would know what she meant.

Waiting for the pain to subside enough so that she could move, Breanne listened for an answering call, a threat, a plea, a beacon to let her know where he was. There was none.

She straightened and took a few quick, cautious steps. Maybe he'd given up trying to stop the baby from being born. Her intense and tentative relief at that possibility was undercoated with sadness, for she knew what that giving up would signify to Greg, what helplessness, what utter vulnerability.

Greg, she told him silently. *I'll be back for you. I'm not abandoning you. I'll never do that. You're my son. My first child.*

Greg. She formed the words deliberately in her mind, though she had no reason to think he'd have understood even if she'd spoken them aloud. *I love you.*

One more corner ahead. Abruptly it seemed to her that dozens, hundreds of corners had somehow developed, that the rectilinear corridor had metamorphosed into a labyrinth. But no, there were the elevators, doors closed.

She stumbled toward them through the assault of another contraction and managed to press the 'Down' button. Obediently, the red, down-pointing triangle above the elevators illuminated.

Breanne leaned heavily against the wall, panting, eyes fixed on the row of round white lights which, very slowly, marked the car's ascent toward her from the lobby. A contraction – a minor one this time, though she'd braced herself for a full-scale onslaught – buzzed through her groin. Hands closed around her arm.

She hadn't seen him. She hadn't heard him. Now she was bathed in his presence, the sheer closeness of him, his terror and his fury. 'Greg!' she shouted. 'The baby!'

The elevator dinged for another floor, but she couldn't see where it was and it didn't matter anymore. She was on the floor, writhing with purposeful pain, struggling to give herself over to the birthing. Greg was kneeling over her. In the dimness of the corridor she couldn't quite see his face, except the faint glistening of his tears.

He collapsed into her, his knees drawn up and his thumb in his mouth. He was keening, a wail so thin and sad that she worried he would need her help to breathe, and knew suddenly that there was not one birthing here but two.

She pulled Greg's head against her, raised her knees, took a deep cleansing breath, exhaled explosively. Greg was nuzzling at her breast; she gave him her fingers to suck, felt the nipping of his teeth, felt the baby plunge forward. Simultaneously, she pushed for the baby and gathered Greg to her. Simultaneously, she screamed with the pain and effort of labor and crooned a lullaby to the half-grown child already a separate person but needing to merge and separate again.

She rubbed Greg's back. He snuggled into her, a boy nearly as big as she was but clearly an infant now. His fingers curled around hers, covering them, having re-discovered the instinct to clutch and to hold on, the trust that she would not let him go.

The baby was partway out, she thought, though she couldn't see it. She felt what seemed an extension of her own body protruding onto the floor, and had a vivid mental image of the birth blood covering Greg's body, too. She panted, trying desperately to remember the prescribed rhythm. Her head swam till she thought she might faint. Vaguely she was aware of the elevator doors opening, pausing, casting a brief bright rectangle of light over her body and the bodies of her children, which were all joined. Then the doors closed and, she supposed, the elevator descended, empty, of no use to them.

'Greg!' she cried. 'Help me!'

With an effort very much like the effort his mother was making beside him, Greg sat up, crouched, watched. His mind held a terrible image of the baby stuck inside his mother forever, of his mother and the baby dying, blowing up, of himself blowing up then, too, because they were all part of each other. He would not let that happen.

He put another picture into his mind. The wall of his mother's birth canal splitting. Just a little. Just enough. He remembered the pictures in the book. Red blood spurting onto his hand, his mother's blood. Things – the right things, the necessary things – breaking, stretching, pulling apart, letting go.

He knew how to do this. He exulted. His mother screamed. He screamed. He saw the baby coming. There was a gurgling sound as the baby slid into the world, into Greg's waiting hands, slippery, bloody, whole and new, safe from him and from Andy. And, like everybody else, with power of its own.